THE WATCHING

THE WATCHING

Paul Melniczek

King's Way Press

King's Way Press
4215 Jimmy Lee Smith
Pkwy Suite #19
Hiram, GA 30141

www.kwp-books.com

ACKNOWLEDGMENTS

The world couldn't have been more wonderful to Pat.

Seeing things through such young eyes, the little girl knew nothing of the cares and vanities of a teen. She simply enjoyed life as it was offered. And it had *much* to offer the cheerful girl.

The warm sunshine outside which smiled down on the house was enough. The sweeping fields of corn which edged the backyard were enough in itself. The crows that flew overhead, squawking and mocking anything they spotted, were enough. The blue sky laced with puffy clouds, where Pat imagined seeing majestic lions parading in the heavens, or hilarious snowmen, up so high they would *surely* melt. Any of these pleasant thoughts could give rise to her infectious giggle, and a smile which went on forever. She loved the country which she called home.

And of course there was her Aunt Margie and Uncle Ray, who had raised Pat since she'd been too little to remember. Ray helped out on the farm bordering their property, while Margie worked as a seamstress in the local mill a few miles away. And when they both were gone, her favorite aunt watched over her,

Trish. Living in the same house with Trish was a dream come true for the small child, since all her 'bestest, people in the world,' as she liked to proclaim, were always near.

Pat and Trish drove the short miles to Kline's Orchard, making the autumn afternoon a minor adventure in itself, as they hand-picked a bushel of apples to bring home. They also picked out several medium-sized pumpkins for carving, as Halloween was the following day. So much stuff going on, the little girl was simply brimming with excitement, squirming in her seat and thinking of all the fun. It was just too much for a child to contain. She felt ready to burst apart at any moment. And her stomach growled like a hungry tomcat. Sweets after supper.

"Apple pie tonight, Aunt Trish?" Pat bit into a piece of fruit so big, all Trish saw were the little green eyes peering over the waxy surface.

"Hmm, how about some juicy apple cobbler instead? With extra cinnamon."

There was the expected pause, and Trish barely concealed a smirk as she gripped the steering wheel, waiting for the girl's reply.

"But that's my *favorite*."

Which was exactly why Trish played the game…

"Or what about some big fat dumplings? With ice cream and milk on top? Yum."

The pause was even longer this time.

"But, you make the bestest apple pie in the world, Aunt Trish."

Now she bit her lip to stop from giggling herself. "I don't know about that. Wouldn't go *that* far. It's all right, I guess." She was really laying it down now. Although sometimes she went overboard, angering even Margie and Ray…"Oh! I know. We'll squeeze 'em and make some apple cider, and keep some just for snacks."

Pat stopped eating her apple, the child's face looking so glum that Trish felt pangs of guilt for teasing her. Trish reached over and took the apple from the little girl's hands, biting a big chunk for herself. Pat's eyes opened wide, her mouth forming an 'O,' and then her aunt laughed. "Apple pie it is, ya' little stinker."

"Yaah…"

"*Unless* you eat all the apples in the bucket."

That quickly the child smiled, and Pat held out her hand palm first until Trish gave the fruit back to her. Then she promptly dropped it back in with the others. "That's to make *sure* I won't. And you tease me too much."

Trish rubbed her head, winking. "But you're so fun to tease. Aw, you know me."

"I do. You're my Aunt Trish."

They both giggled.

The three of them sat down in the small dining room, digging into the meat and potatoes, although Pat couldn't resist peering into the kitchen between forkfuls, trying to catch a glimpse of Trish's baking. The smell of apples was strong and pleasant. The mahogany table was an antique, along with most of their other furniture. A shelf sat in one corner, made by Ray years ago. It comfortably held a number of plates and other accompanying pieces of cookware, some brightly colored in red and green for the holidays.

Ray and Margie had their 'feet planted squarely in the ground,' as local folk would say. Mundane and traditional, they were kindly and practical people, with a love of family and country which ran through their blood.

Pat looked overhead at the flickering candle wicks on the pressed tin chandelier. The autumn nights arrived earlier each evening, and they used candles throughout the house to conserve electricity. Sconces adorned most of the walls, holding fat beeswax tapers. Pat thought it was 'kinda' neat and sort of scary' sometimes, but she was used to it.

Ray scratched his right shoulder where his overalls tended to rub, a grimace on his wrinkled face.

"Are they too tight? I told you to let me fix that for you earlier."

"Umhh." It wasn't exactly a word, but around the house it served the same purpose.

Pat understood Margie's remark immediately. Although it sounded like a question, it was really her aunt's way of scolding her husband, who usually took the short cut when it came to such things. Like adjusting his clothing…Margie caught the knowing look on the girl's face, and shot her a quick wink.

"That uncle of yours. Why, the other week he insisted on wearing his new boots all day at the farm, and rubbed his heels open until they were bleeding. Came hobbling home like he'd been riding on a mule for the whole afternoon."

Ray pretended to ignore the comment, but the two females laughed at his expense.

"Is that true Uncle Ray?"

He scowled at his plate, causing Pat to hold one hand over her mouth as she tried to contain the laugh coming from inside.

"Your Aunt Margie likes to pick on me, honey. This poor old farmer works himself into the ground all day long, and then he has to come home and put up with her torment."

"Ha, old farmer my behind...And who else would put up with you if it wasn't me? Cleaning stinky pig mud from socks cause' he fell into the drainage pit? Or cow manure from his boots from not paying attention to where he's walking? Pat, dear. When you grow up, make sure you marry someone who isn't so clumsy, okay?"

Ray grumbled something beneath his breath and stood up, heading for the kitchen, but before he went even two feet he received another warning. "And if you poke at your sister's apple pie before it cools, you'll be getting all crust."

With that, the girls smiled conspiratorially and continued eating.

Pat peered over the rim of her blankets, yawning. It was one of those nights when she just couldn't sleep. She looked over at the mouse-faced clock on the wall. The hands were like oversize mittens, goofy and 'cartoony,' as she called them. One was on the twelve, the other after. It was pretty late, she knew, well past everyone's bedtime. Ray worked long hours, and Margie was up early in the morning, getting breakfast ready and doing all the little things 'which needed doin',' as she always said.

Crawling from the warm covers, Pat walked over to the window and stared outside. It looked spooky out there, she thought. The moon was bright and round, splashing the corn fields below in pale silver. The tall stalks trembled in the wind, and Pat shivered just a bit herself. She had always been a bit scared of the dark. Not terrified like a very young child could be when left alone—after all, she was not a little girl anymore. *She* thought so, at least.

No, this was more insidious, subtle. Something inside of her was nervous, thinking about all the old fairy tales, about things which supposedly came out after the sun went down, chasing after naughty little children. She knew they were just stories, about the boogeyman, ghosts, witches, and stuff like that. And that's exactly what they were. Stories. Meant to scare *naughty* kids, or they were good for listening at night from an adult, especially this time of year, with Halloween only a day or two away. Fun and scary, *except* when the grownups were off in another part of the house, and you had trouble sleeping at night... Aunt Trish loved to tell her spooky stories, and Pat would hang on her every word, holding her breath, her eyes growing wider by the sentence. But at the end, Trish would laugh and hug her niece, telling her it was all made up. And Pat knew it.

But she had scared her worse than ever earlier that day, and Pat had run off to the basement in anger and fear. Trish came after her apologizing, but not until the girl was hugged and consoled, a promise made not to do it again. It hadn't been a fun afternoon.

Pat did a lot of thinking, and sometimes her imagination had its own...what? Imagination? That didn't make any sense. Pat wondered about the word *imagination*. She could picture it being a thing alive, a furry little man who slept inside of her mind. Maybe it was like her, and had trouble sleeping at times, and would wake up. Like right now, as she looked across the fields, thinking scary thoughts.

She frowned, sticking her nose against the glass. It was cold, and she pressed harder. Backing up, she looked at the imprint as it slowly disappeared. Was that how ghosts disappeared?

There she was again, thinking something spooky! Another chill raced her spine, like a spider scurrying for cover. It was all

Aunt Trish's fault. She'd scared her to death earlier, and Pat hated the feeling she'd had afterwards. She loved her aunt, but sometimes she picked on her too much. Pat shook her head, trying to shake away bad thoughts.

Yeah, her imagination was wide awake tonight…Pat and her invisible friend. She liked to think of everything as her friends. The two cats that roamed the house were some, of course. Whiskers and Katy. Plus the animals on the farm where her uncle worked, and just about anything else Pat saw outside. The birds, groundhogs, deer, possums, raccoons, frogs by the pond, the occasional box turtle or two, but they were out mostly in the late spring, for some reason. Anyway, it was a lot easier living in a friendly world. Thinking about the turtles made her smile, and she pushed open the window halfway, enjoying the brisk air against her warm face.

But her eyes popped wide as she heard a voice somewhere below her in the night. Immediately her skin went cold, and all the scary thoughts roared up in her mind as if a door had sprung open.

She swallowed, her throat suddenly parched. There it was again, a voice! But who would be out there, this late at night? Cautiously, she strained her neck and looked down. The sound came from right beneath her. Pat's room sat on the second floor, and it offered an open view to their backyard and the fields beyond. Then she recognized her aunt's voice. Trish was outside, but doing what? Talking to someone? Wait, she heard her doing an imitation, of…a cat. Trish whistled, slapping her hand. She was out there calling one of the cats, that was all! Sometimes the rascals scratched at the door if they were out late, and Pat remembered waking up already, hearing them herself. Trish was a light sleeper, though, and sometimes stayed up into the night reading books, or drinking something warm in the kitchen to help her get sleepy. Pat didn't know if any of these worked, but she knew what it felt like when she couldn't sleep either. Like right *now*…

She stuck her head out further, attempting to catch a glimpse of her aunt. It was a clear autumn night, and the moon was a pale reflection of its daytime counterpart, but Pat could still make out figures below. Small bushes surrounded parts of the large porch, and with her nose poking at the window screen, she snatched a peek at Trish, bent down to the ground, trying to manage what looked to be a very stubborn cat. Pat listened to the low voice…

"C'mon, you bugger. Drive me nuts scratching at the door, and now you don't want to come in. Psss psss…here pusser."

Pat smirked. She couldn't help it. Served Trish right for scaring her earlier… Those darn cats could be so fussy! She thought it was probably Whiskers, who had an unpredictable personality. Loveable most of the time, he could at any moment spring away as if being chased by a hundred dogs, and for no apparent reason. And other times, both animals acted weird. Even her Uncle Ray commented on their strange behavior. They would stare at the walls for long minutes, even for an hour or more, watching. Trish blamed it on the mice, but Pat already had laid on the hardwood floor next to one of them, even pasted her ear against the wall, listening for any telltale sounds. She never heard a thing. Not a scratch, nothing scurrying within the paneling. Her uncle said cats could hear things that people couldn't, so it wasn't any surprise. Disappointment, but no surprise…Trish would joke, and said maybe there were ghosts in the walls. Although she always laughed about it, Pat was left feeling uneasy. She didn't like the idea of spooks roaming their home, even as a joke. That word, imagination again…

Pat remembered the little sing-song she'd made up in her head whenever she was feeling scared.

No ghosts, no goblins, no monsters, just me.

No ghosts, no goblins, no monsters, just me!

It was nothing spectacular, no catchy rhyme or melody attached, but something to fall back on and make her think, at the very least. It always worked, so there...

Below, Trish was still trying to coax the reluctant cat. Pat shook her head. What a naughty tabby it was being tonight. Her aunt stood up, and said something under her breath, which Pat didn't want to repeat.

Then her head snapped up. She ignored the cat and looked around, as if searching for something. Pat felt chills scuttle along her spine and she followed Trish's gaze. Maybe there was an animal walking around in the yard. Nothing unusual there...

But Trish stepped backwards, and then stopped. This time, Pat heard it too. It was...well, weird sounding. She tried to place what it could be, but wasn't sure. She tilted her head so that her hearing would be better. There it was again! It sounded like creaking—no, too long for that. Almost as if something was being stretched out, bent. That was the only way Pat could describe it now. And it wasn't very loud, but soft. She peered down at her aunt, and what Pat saw terrified her even more. For whatever was causing the noise did not come from the yard, but *behind* her, in the house itself.

The girl held her breath, feeling a rush of excitement and fear.

For one second Trish stood with her arms held high, and then the next she was *pulled away*, as something grabbed her.

The young girl watched with mouth wide open, too stunned to move, shout, even think. Aunt Trish was out of her view, and the night was silent once again. But *too* silent, as if the entire world had shrunken, slunk away to hide. In that moment, Pat knew that something terrible had happened to her aunt. Something monstrous. Her hands trembled and she wet herself. Her eyes watered and her throat felt so fat she couldn't swallow.

And that was how her Aunt Margie found her several hours later.

Tim put his feet down, stopping his bike. The air was brisk, but he liked it. When the sun shone like it did now, and the air had that tangy sharpness of fall to it, *then* you felt alive. Really alive. He loved it all. Of course, he was a perpetual optimist for the most part, and it was part of his nature.

He looked at the house, his face curious.

I wonder what she does by herself, living alone there.

He had to admit, he didn't know that much about Pat anymore. Except that she was the only one living there right now. Besides an occasional wave as he passed by, that was the extent of their contact. They were the same age, and had attended school together. Himself, the talkative boy with a smile always nearby. Pat, the shy girl, with the pixie face, short auburn hair, and sad brown eyes. To his recollection, Tim had probably been her only real friend. The school was your typical rural one, very small and close-knit. Everyone knew everyone else, and the talk of the day revolved around the weather, crops, and whose animal was running away, or what did Marvin the butcher have on sale this week.

Tim loved his home. Despite his own unfortunate past, he wouldn't trade his life for anything. But he *was* lonely, there was no doubt. He never had a girlfriend, and to be honest, there weren't too many local girls that struck his interest. And for some reason, many of the farmer's wives gave birth overwhelmingly to sons, which was fine by the farmers, truth be told. A young boy grew up to be a young man, and could help their father run the land. Sure, there were a few girls, but Tim just shook his head, thinking about them. *Dolly* certainly had a crush on him. But if she continued to gain weight and turn out like her mother, she would need to be hauled around in a wheel barrow when she got older.

Tim bit his lip, feeling guilty at the unkind thought, but couldn't get the vision of her out of his mind, with himself toting her around the yard in a rusty metal wheel barrow. *Be nice now…*

His mom would have scolded him good if she knew what he was thinking. But she wouldn't know. Or, rather, if she *did* know, she probably wouldn't be able to tell him. His parents had died several years ago in a car accident while driving home from town on a foggy night. Tim was supposed to have gone along, but stayed home with a cold. And that had probably saved his life.

He frowned, replaying the events of that following morning when he learned the terrible news. He sighed deeply, staring up at the sky. "I miss you guys. But I know you're in good hands." With such devastation in his past, Tim was a remarkable young man indeed. His outlook on life remained positive, and he continued on, day by day, being as productive as possible. But he longed to be close to Pat, someone who had to be as lonely as himself, considering her own personal tragedy. So Tim had recently decided to make his move. The annual harvest dance was coming soon, and he was going to ask Pat to go with him. His palms felt moist just at the thought…He would ask her soon. This weekend at latest. He fancied her looking out the window even now, seeing him on his bike, staring inside at her. A chance meeting was *not* what he had in mind, though. It could be extremely uncomfortable…or just maybe the opportunity he was looking for. But he didn't feel quite ready.

Soon, but not just yet.

He whistled, and rode away.

Pat worked in the garden, unaware of Tim's scrutiny as he paused before her house. She plucked at the last crop of tomatoes, well-past their prime, but still good enough to bring about a few dollars at her roadside stand, which brought in most of her income. It wasn't the easiest way to survive, living off the land and the last of her aunt and uncle's savings, but it was all she had.

All she could do.

She bent down, looking over the large, round pumpkins, which lay sprawled out, their orange skin a dull reflection of the midday sun. They were ready to be picked. She had always loved pumpkins, and Halloween, since she was a young child. The spooky holiday. But the appeal had worn off over the years, reduced to a celebration of habit now, like everything else. Another lusterless holiday, another season, another month, another week, another day, another night…

Her loneliness was a beast in itself. Something that was

an unwelcome companion, constantly sidling along with her. It shadowed her the day long while she kept to the household chores. It whispered in Pat's mind, casting a gloomy pall over other emotions which were denied to her. When was the last time she'd smiled at anything? Pat couldn't remember. When she stared in the mirror, sad eyes returned the gaze. Modest, she knew her youthful, girlish looks hadn't changed too much. But the eyes... yes. The eyes told the truth, and they spoke of someone haunted. Aging inside. Her face and body were young, but her heart and mind were aging quickly. The constant stress of her life was extraordinary. How had she lasted this long?

Because she had been permitted to. Nothing more, nothing less. The reason? She didn't know. Maybe there was no reason, no active thought. Only a deep-seated malice, which at any time could burst forth, the rage consuming someone close to her. Her Aunt Trish. Margie and Ray. Victims all. When would her time come?

She felt chills at the thought, and she glanced over at the house. But slowly, with great care, not focusing her mind on the truth. Instead, to a chance observer, she might be looking at the vines which needed trimming at the sides. Or examining the spouting which needed cleaning. Or the back porch, in need of repair. Or the thick shrubs which should be pruned back.

The compost pile which needed turning.

The grass could be cut once more this year.

Windows cleaned and winterized.

Storm door fixed.

Shutters painted.

More...

Leaves fell everyday in sweeps of burnt orange and yellow. They need raking. There was always so much to do. But that was good.

Anything which kept her busy.

And especially outside the house.

Most of all, not watching.

For something…

Pat swallowed, her throat dry. She could use a cool glass of water. There was a well located on the property, and it was always reliable, having never run out. Not even three summers ago when the drought had ravished the surrounding farmland like a retreating army scorching the earth. People who lived in the country were a different breed, in communion with nature and the things they touched, smelled, tasted. It was the same here. There was a definite relationship Pat had with her land —she cared for all its needs, and it cared for her right back.

She absently rubbed her hands along the nearest pumpkin's shiny surface, looking for bumps and blemishes. There were none. Its coating was flawless, as she knew it would be. As all the others would be. They always were.

She pulled a small knife from her pocket, gently cutting the vine at the stem and freeing the pumpkin. Hefting it in her hands, she carried it over to the picnic table, which had not seen any picnics for several years. Only her presence. She remembered the flowers she had picked once from the field, decorating the table for an afternoon frolic with her aunt and uncle. Fresh apple and peach pies, homemade lemonade, burgers on the grill, city chicken on sticks…

And when they had left her alone for a minute to grab some more food from the kitchen, Pat had put the finishing touches on her makeshift bouquet, adding a bluebell here, a daisy there, a wisteria bloom from the arbor. She'd stepped back, admiring her handiwork. A nice display for her simple court, she thought, nodding her head with satisfaction at the time.

And the table had writhed before her eyes like an agitated snake…

Pat shuddered, banishing the terrible memory from her head. She couldn't afford to dwell on such things. Not now, not ever. Keep busy, she told herself. Pay attention to your work. Try not to think too much.

And don't watch.

"Thirty-five dollars, and some odd cents." Tim mumbled to himself as he counted the day's take from his own roadside stand. "Eh, not too bad, I guess."

He looked up as a vehicle approached, recognizing it immediately as Sheriff Ron Kramer's Crown Victoria police cruiser. The car slowed, then pulled onto the loose gravel in front of the modest structure, which was little more than half a shack with a wooden roof overhead which protected against the elements. Tim had built it himself a few years ago, deciding to make some extra money by putting out his vegetables and other assorted items. On any given day from late spring until fall, the shelves were filled with tomatoes, peppers, onions, watermelon, corn, squash, and a slew of other offerings, depending on the weather and what rotation schedule Tim was currently working with.

"Hey Tim, how's it going?"

"Fine, Sheriff. Not a bad haul. Care for a few tomatoes?"

Ron got out of the car, shaking his head politely. "No thanks. Later this week I'll check some stuff out. I still have a full vegetable drawer at home."

"Sure. But the season's almost over, you know. Hard to believe, isn't it?"

"Yeah." The sheriff adjusted his hat, looking across the long fields of corn which surrounded Tim's house and barn, a sea of faded yellow, several sections already cut down. "Things working out all right with Jason yet?"

"Uh-huh." Jason was the neighboring farmer who leased most of Tim's land. "I'll be on my own in another two or three years, I figure. Hopefully less. There's a lot to learn, but I'm getting there."

"I'll bet." Ron leaned lazily against the car, scratching his chin. "I was never cut out for that kinda' work. For me, it was either off to college and some business degree, or find another way to stay around here and make a living. Can't complain." Ron was around forty five years old, and pretty solid. The relatively quiet community had not softened him at all. He was several inches over six foot, and close to two hundred and fifty pounds. Enough to make nearly anyone in the county think twice about giving him any problems...There were very few.

"Decorate for Halloween yet? Still have some fine pumpkins in the field. Sold a couple, but a lot of people wait until the day before."

"Not yet, but Rhonda's been bugging me. So have the twins…" The sheriff laughed. "Funny time of year. Used to be pretty crazy, mostly kids out having a good time, pranks and stuff. But there's little tolerance anymore. The world's a different place, even here in Grainersville. You wouldn't know it though. Folks around here stick to their business and just do their thing. That's why I stayed."

Tim nodded. "You're right. I've had plenty of reasons to leave myself. But I just can't." He was silent for a moment, the sheriff waiting respectfully for him to continue. "I love it here.

It's my home, and it will always be my home. My parents settled here, saved up for the farm, and I made a promise years ago that I'd make it work. No matter what." He stared at Ron, and the sheriff patted him on the arm.

"You've got a good head on your shoulders. You're doing just fine, boy. Don't change at all. You'll make a full-blown farmer pretty soon."

"That's what I've been hearing." He grinned. "Thanks for the support." On a whim, he decided to ask the sheriff something else, without giving away his feelings though. "Rode past the Kucher house earlier. Do you ever talk to Pat? She never seems to go out anywhere."

The sheriff's face grew dark. "That's a real shame there." He paused. "The few times I run into her, she's always polite, but quiet. Really quiet. I just wonder if what happened to her family is going to haunt her for the rest of her life. I don't know that I could have been that strong...Damn shame. It's amazing that she carries on so well."

Tim was uncomfortable, immediately regretting bringing up the subject.

Ron continued, shaking his head now. "She must be awfully lonely living there by herself. I feel sorry for her. But I don't know what to do. You have to give her some room, I respect that. But there's a lot of friendly folks around here. I think they'd welcome her, if she ever broke out of her shell, that is. But what happened to her family has to be the biggest mystery in the county."

They both looked up as another car approached. It was moving pretty fast but slowed down, the driver obviously seeing the police cruiser. Tim recognized it as Joe Harper's blue Nova, the mag tires and loud engine giving it away even before it reached them. The pair watched as the car rumbled past them, Ron eye-ing the car suspiciously. Joe was driving, of course, and someone else sat in the passenger seat. Had to be Sam Wixel, thought Tim. His best friend. *Only* friend.

Despite his carefree nature, Tim disliked both of them heart-ily, for good reason. Their reputations were well-known in the area.

The sheriff muttered. "Punks…Ah, well. I guess every town has their share. Nothing but trouble. Small-time stuff. I know they're behind most of the problems, but I can't finger them yet."

"I suppose so." Tim agreed, turning back to his stand, his good mood suddenly soured.

"Gotta' go. Maybe I can spook those two on my way back to town." Ron's grin was less humor and more attitude. Tim knew the man pretty well.

"Have a good one, sheriff. And don't wait too long for the pumpkins."

"Evening, Tim. And hey, you sound a lot like my wife now." He chuckled, ducking back into his car.

Tim waved, then returned to his work. It was getting dark outside, and he wanted to finish up here and do some more things around the farm. He never dwelled on the countless chores needed to maintain the property. To anyone else, it would have been a daunting prospect—inheriting it all while still in his late teens, and remarkably, being able to keep things under con-trol. True, leasing out part of the fields was a big help, but that still left a mountain of other things to take care of. He'd been ap-proached by several others immediately after the tragic accident, but held firm. He *could* manage, and no, the property was not for sale. Not now, not ever. There were opportunists everywhere, and even now, some waited for him to slip up, or simply admit defeat, announce that he was cashing in and moving out.

But these people did not know Tim, and were definitely not his friends. In Tim's opinion, these type of folks *had* no real friends except for ones that you could put in the bank or your wallet.

After several minutes, Tim was ready to head back to the house. He still had his bicycle with him, and despite the fact that he already owned a reliable Ford pickup, he enjoyed just riding around on short errands, moving constantly between the road stand and his own house. Also, town was only a few short miles away, and making the trip on two wheels made him feel a little closer to Pat as he peddled past. He only wished she felt the same about him.

Pat sat at the kitchen table, sipping from a cup of hot tea. Actually, her favorite drink this time of year was spiced apple cider, and she could find some at the general store in town, or Prescott's Orchard, which sold tons of apples and other related items like pies, baked goods, and local produce.

But she didn't leave the house very often, and never for too long. It wasn't a good idea, and she was terrified of something happening.

She sat there, lost in thought, thinking of the past and the strange things which were all part of her daily life. How had she managed through the years and still maintained her sanity? Had she survived strictly on her courage? Or maybe something beyond that, something which enabled her to move from one fearful day to the next? She dared not think too much about it. Even forming this word in her mind was painful. It was magic to her, an elusive strand of enchantment that hovered on the edge of reality and fantasy, beckoned to Pat within daydreams and during the occasional bliss of undisturbed sleep that didn't include the phantoms of her existence. This word was a concept that had long been denied her, but she refused to let it go entirely.

Hope.

A simple, beautiful word. A wondrous word. And seeking hope could raise one from the deepest abyss, bring them higher out of despair, and overcome incredible obstacles set before them. But her situation was different. More of a fairytale than anything else, rooted in things which defied rationalization. There was no one she could turn to for help. In the past, she had considered running outside in desperation, screaming at the top of her lungs, to tell someone, *anyone...*

Who could help? The police, doctors, clergy? None of them...They would lock her away, institutionalize her, and others would get hurt because of her. And *that* was the single worst fear which plagued the girl. She didn't want anyone else dragged into her world. Everyone had nightmares, but Pat's happened to be real. It wasn't fair to bring it onto someone else, although she longed for companionship. Nightmares were of a singular nature, and such demons were not to be shared. Especially if they could be awakened, and had a life of their own.

Pat blinked, realizing how deeply she had drifted into this line of thought. She caught herself staring at the wall, and immediately shifted her gaze. Stare too long, and *something* might happen.

A chill slithered across her back, cold fingers spider-walking up and down her spine. She knew from experience that the dormancy could be disturbed just by her undivided attention. It had happened before. It was another terrible revelation she'd learned years ago after the deaths of her aunt and uncle. There existed a connection between herself and *them*. She didn't have a name for it, as there was no definition for something so horrific and unexplainable. And she had tried without success to unlock the secret, pry into corners and shadows, but carefully, *oh* so carefully. It wasn't easy, and at times she felt the agitation ripple through the house, the undercurrent of tension and dread, and worst of all, *watchfulness*.

As unobtrusively as possible, indirectly, Pat watched for them. And there was no way of knowing when they were watching *her*...

Stop, she told herself. Don't dwell on it.

But how could she not? She needed to learn something about them, what gave them life, purpose. And terrible as it sounded, she realized she might never understand, that maybe there was no motivation to their existence. And there could be no ending to it all.

And that was why Pat tried not to listen to her mind too much when the word hope called softly to her.

The house was dark and quiet, a single light on upstairs. Dusk had fallen, washing the landscape in pale silver beneath a harvest moon. A few tattered clouds scuttled across the sky, ushered away by a growing wind. The country road was deserted, a speck of light coming from the next farmhouse half a mile away.

"Creepy place."

"Kind of…yeah, it is. *She* is too."

"Hmm. But she's cute, for a weirdo."

Smug laughter, but not humorous. Not in the least.

"You're serious then? About breaking inside?"

"Yeah. I am." There was no hesitation in the voice. "Bet she's never had a boyfriend either. I know she hasn't. I remember her in school, never talking to anyone. Couldn't meet you in the eyes, if you know what I mean. Like she was hiding something."

"Maybe she is."

"Could be," Joe Harper replied, and turned to look over at Sam Wixel, whose small, narrow eyes bore a striking resemblance to those of a pig. Joe could have said the same comment about his own friend never having a girlfriend, but it wasn't worth it. He had other things on his mind at the moment.

Joe turned his gaze back to the house. "I think she's hiding something—a naughty girl with a big bad secret. Bad girl...And she needs to be taught a lesson."

Sam sniggered, and Joe found the noise annoying.

"Ain't nothing *funny* about it, Sam."

His friend immediately shut up.

"Matter of fact, I'm not sure I can even trust you. No one can ever know about this, if she decides to talk. I don't think she will though. But...if we get caught, we'll both be dead meat."

"Do you think she will?" Joe saw the steam from Sam's heavy breathing in the cool air.

"Nah. Just keep your mask on when we start. I think she'll just stay locked up in that weird old house of hers for the rest of her life. I'm not too worried though... Think about it. It's not like we're doing anything that shouldn't have been done before. It'll be punishment. I *know* she killed her family. People around here are dumb enough to be fooled, but not me. Who disappears like that without a trace? C'mon..."

"But they never found anything. Everybody pities her." Sam's voice shook from excitement.

"Well, not me, that's for damn sure. Who knows, maybe she'll even tell us the real truth, about how she did it." This time it was Joe who laughed—a nasty, spiteful, overconfident laugh. Sam joined in, but lower and more uncertain.

"You ready?" The stocky youth moved forward, his silhouette bearish in the dim light. His eagerness was evident, and he hunched down, huffing.

Joe snagged him by his sweatshirt. "Not yet, you idiot. We'll wait for the right time. Until the day before Halloween, maybe... Seems like the best time of the year to catch a naughty little witch."

Sam groaned, disappointed, but said nothing.

"And don't you open that fat mouth of yours to anyone, hear me?" Joe grabbed him with both hands, his lean frame moving catlike in the dark. "Understand? Or else you'll end up in jail, or worse. A lot worse, believe me."

"I won't, you know I won't, Joe. Give me a break."

Joe stared at him, unmoving. After several long moments, he nodded. "I know you won't, Sam. We're in this together. Let's go."

They slipped back into the shadows towards Joe's Nova.

Within the house, something stirred.

To anyone looking, nothing would have seemed out of place. There were no windows slamming shut by an invisible hand, doors were not opening or closing on their own, pictures did not have shifty eyes. The temperature did not become cold, or even warm. There was no noise accompanying this change of state, no rotten stench belying its existence. The television did not react in static agitation, lights did not blink on and off, appliances did not switch modes without explanation. Animals might have noticed due to their refined senses and instincts, but there were no pets inside the house. There had been several in past years, but they were no more.

But there *was* activity, at a level so minute as to be unseen by people, unnoticeable to all except for perhaps the most extremely sensitive of the gifted. It was like the easing of pressure beneath a mountain range, a gentle sighing, an unshakable, elemental force, both natural and subtle, and at the same time so fantastic that it defied definition or comprehension. It was invisible by choice, but had sentience. Most of the time it slumbered, lost in a black oblivion far removed from the waking thoughts of mankind. It slept in such a fashion, unaware of the mundane trappings of the 'normal' world. The world of flesh and blood. It saw, but without eyes. It heard, without ears. It *knew* of the comings and goings around it, although emotions were as alien to its consciousness as it was to human feelings.

For a passing of time, it had been dormant, dwelling within its chosen place of habitat.

And now, it had become restless again.

It was Friday morning, and Tim stood before Pat's house with sweaty palms. He bit his lip, trying to fight back his nerves.

Well, here I am at last. Man, this is tougher than I thought. Like a darn schoolboy. Jeez…

He swallowed several times, and steadied his breathing. He felt disappointed in himself for reacting like this.

It's only a date, not the end of the world. The worst that can happen is she'll say no, and thank me for asking. I hope she don't though.

But he didn't want to go home with that answer ringing in his ears. Tim was a humble young man, but like everyone else, had feelings, and this was a very personal undertaking. Pretty much a first for him. So gathering his courage, he stepped on to the front porch, which was swept clean, a small round table sitting in the middle. Decorating it were several gourds, and two pumpkins, neither of them carved. The place certainly was neat, well-maintained. He liked that, since he was about as industrious as anyone else around. His mother had always quoted to him that 'idle time is the devil's work.' Tim tended to agree. When someone had too much free time, they became bored and lazy. And that opened the door for mischief with some folk. Not all, but some.

He lifted his hand, ready to knock, but was startled by a voice.

"Oh…"

Tim snapped his head to the side and there stood Pat carrying a small paper bag and holding a pair of hedge clippers. It was hard to tell who seemed more surprised at the abrupt meeting.

"Pat?" He immediately felt foolish at the startled tone in his own voice. It *was* her house, after all. Who did he expect to be here?

"Tim? Uh, hello, what do you want?"

He stammered, walking over to her.

Might as well get right to the point. Here goes nothing…

"Hi, it's good to see you, Pat. You look great. Why, I came over to ask if you wanted to go to the dance with me." He felt a bit more confident when the words were finally spoken, and he managed a warm smile on top of it. But her reaction shocked him. She looked as if she'd just seen a ghost, and remained standing there, her mouth wide open. After a few seconds, his confidence melted, and he felt his cheeks blush furiously in embarrassment. What a fool, he thought. She's not interested in me at all!

He looked down at his boots, and wished he'd never set foot on her porch. All his pleasant fantasies about making Pat his girlfriend had vanished, leaving only a black, empty pit in the middle of his stomach. He couldn't have felt any lower. She still had not replied, and Tim seriously wondered if she held a secret grudge against him that he didn't know about. Maybe something he'd done to her in school? But he wasn't aware of anything. And the few times he would pass her house and she happened to be out, Pat had always waved to him, seeming friendly enough.

"Tim, I, don't know what to say…"

He looked up and met her eyes, and in those brown orbs Tim saw a reflection of his own emotion. Loneliness. A glimmer of hope, for companionship. There was a longing inside of this girl that he saw and *felt*. And the intensity of it was quite unexpected. She then quickly glanced over at the house, her eyes shifting slightly, as if looking for someone, but not wanting to draw attention. Tim followed her gaze, half-expecting to see someone his own age suspiciously watching the both of them, but the windows were all blocked, the curtains drawn tight.

"I can't go with you…"

Her voice was hushed, the words seeping out like spring rain dripping onto a meadow; sad, gentle.

"You can't?" Tim was crushed. Confused. Her eyes told him yes, he was sure of it. But something held her back.

"I'll pay for you, of course. Or…do you have a boyfriend?" He was hoping her answer was 'no' for the second question. *That* would really hurt. If Pat was seeing someone already, then Tim had waited too long in asking her out, and would have to live with his hesitation. Yeah, that would be tough.

"No, I don't have a boyfriend." She answered shyly, her head dipping down, and it was her turn to look uncomfortable. "I just can't go, that's all."

Tim frowned, at a total loss as to his next action. He was not very good at this type of thing—he would be the first to admit. Give him household chores, a cow to milk, fields to work, a fence to paint, and a million other tasks, and he would get the job done, and do it right. But girls were quite another challenge, and he was not up to it. He decided to cut his losses and give her an opening…

"All right, but if you change your mind, call me, or stop by the farm." He felt a bit bolder, despite his disappointment. "And I won't ask anyone else, just in case you do. I can always find something at home anyway. Maybe watch a scary movie for Halloween, you know?" He shrugged, trying to smile, but it came out awkward, and he again felt like a fool.

Pat flinched when he mentioned a scary movie, her eyes narrowing. "I'd like to go with you, Tim…" She paused, fidgeting. "Actually, you've been the closest thing to a friend that I can remember. But I just can't."

The rejection hurt, and Tim was puzzled by the mixed signals he both saw and heard. Strange, to say the least.

"Well, that's all right then, I understand…" But he *didn't*. "If you change your mind, give me a call. Gotta' go, plenty of stuff to do at home. Nice talking to you again, Pat. Bye."

He turned, stepping lightly off the porch and walking towards his bicycle. He never looked back.

Pat sat in the wooden rocking chair, her eyes boring into the pages. Reading the book.

Not reading the book…

She blinked, realizing that she'd scanned over the same paragraph at least three times already, maybe more, and couldn't for the life of her have explained anything she'd read. It wasn't the first time this had happened, and certainly wouldn't be the last time. She loved reading. It was an escape from her isolated reality. A fairytale island where the sun always shown, warm and friendly. Waves crashed hypnotically against bright sands of pure white. Everything was open and wonderful, not a house in sight. She longed for such freedom, but was frightened to make an attempt at pursuing the dream. And today, a tiny speck of hope had glimmered at her, but she'd extinguished it.

Tim.

She'd always liked Tim in school, and although his appearance surprised her, the fact that he asked her out had not. Unexpected, perhaps, but not a shock. And such a simple thing, for her to go with him and attend the annual Halloween harvest dance at the town hall. To anyone else, a fun but mundane activity, requiring little thought or preparation. But for Pat, it was a decision which could have disastrous consequences. Maybe even life or death.

Again, she stared at the words, letting the ink blur together as her eyes absorbed the paper. This was an old game. A tired, old act.

Distraction.

Misdirection.

Several names applied, all pointing to the same purpose. A constant attempt at appeasement. Focus her attention on everything else, and not the house itself. Prevent a recurrence. There had been no activity for a long time. Not even a hint in the past two years. This dormancy gave her that small piece of hope which she dared hang onto. And now Tim had visited her, asking her to the dance. It broke her heart, denying his request. His face, so sad.

Pat sighed, a wash of mental and physical fatigue. She closed her eyes, thinking, thinking…

Maybe. Just maybe, it was time.

For a test.

See her limitations.

There were no fences barring her passage to the outside world. No marked boundaries, lines drawn across field or road. But there existed a prison of sorts. And she didn't need to see ropes or chains to understand this. Her house was the cage with unlocked doors, and the home had keepers. The world outside was a vast frontier, and she had only but *tasted* the freedom offered there. Short trips were exhilarating and frightening at the same time. Only *she* understood this. To the outside world, there was nothing to be seen. But to Pat, it was different. Oh, yes.

She agonized. Glanced at the phone. Looked at the book. Tilted her head to the side. Rubbed her forehead. Looked at the phone again. The book.

The phone. Shut her eyes tightly. Sobbed.

Again her eyes opened, snapping wide.

Yes. She would try it…

Test the house. The possible consequences were terrifying, and the last thing she wanted was to endanger anyone else, Tim most of all. But nothing bad had ever happened *outside* the house, to her recollection. A few warnings years ago, yes. But she really didn't think Tim would be hurt. If she thought there was even the slightest chance, then she wouldn't dare to go down this road.

But the current road would eventually lead to madness, or worse. Wasn't that a more terrible fate than never trying? Giving up, admitting defeat? Maybe there *was* a way to fight back. But she would never find it while remaining totally isolated from the outside world. She was maturing, a young woman. Not a terrified little girl, or even teenager. Yes, she was still scared down to her very soul at times. But she had changed over the years. Living with so much fear had hardened Pat—to some degree, at least.

And it was time for her to act on this small pebble of courage, before it was too late.

She stood, and carefully picked up the telephone book. Flipped through the pages until she found his number, then carefully scratched it down on a note pad. She stared at the number for a while, once even reaching gingerly for the phone, but stopping just short. She felt a bead of sweat on her forehead, clammy hands slinking along her back. It would be incredibly difficult. Having come even to this point, she was unsure if she would be able to go through all the way.

Pat backed away, slumping into the chair once more. She needed to muster up her courage, maybe give herself some more time. She grabbed the book, moving to the page marker and picking up where she left off.

And didn't understand a word she read.

4

Tim had kept busy the past few days, trying not to think about his encounter with Pat, her refusal to his offer, and the girl's subsequent odd reaction. With a million things to take care of, Tim had plenty to occupy himself with besides the disappointing episode.

But still he couldn't shake it from his mind.

He pulled up to the town hall in his pickup. It was a cloudy day, and tomorrow was Halloween, so he was donating some of his field pumpkins to the annual harvest dance. He walked up the steps to the side of the building and tried the door, finding it open, which was no surprise. He chanced a glance inside, but it was dark, and he fumbled for the light switch panel to his right. Flicking them on, the high overheads revealed a typical firehall, with wood flooring, tables filling the center, a bar in the far corner, and a stage to the left end. Boxes and containers were piled on the buffet tables to the other side, and people had already been at work setting up decorations, but there was a lot more to be done before the event. Tim went back outside, shivering against the brisk air. He made several trips carrying the pumpkins, placing them against the near wall. Saving the largest one for last, he gasped, setting it gently down on the floor, and nearly jumped his skin as something slapped him on the back.

He turned in surprise, then shook his head when he recognized Mayor Grimley's red face. The stout man had his characteristic roguish grin plastered from ear to ear.

"Boo! Looks like I gave you an early Halloween scare, son."

"Yeah you did... Hopefully the last, too."

The mayor laughed, a deep throaty sound that announced his presence from half a room away. "Ah, well. It's a fun time of the year, Tim. It's all about having fun, and giving a good scare now and then. I have a few tricks up my sleeve for this year, just you wait and see. Oh, here's a pair of free tickets for donating the pumpkins. Save you ten bucks, and I appreciate your generosity."

He pulled the tickets from his pocket, but Tim frowned. "Don't know if I'm coming tomorrow."

"What? Why not? You better come, you were there last year, if I remember—and don't be such a couch potato. You'll never find a nice woman for a wife if you don't socialize more, boy."

Tim shook his head, a bit embarrassed. "I *was* hoping to go, but got turned down."

"Hmm, that's too bad. Love is a strange game. You win some, you lose some. But there's plenty of girls out there who have an eye for you, Tim. That one girl, what's her name..." He muttered for a moment. "Got it! Dolly Winkle. She's always talking up a storm about you from what I hear."

Tim groaned softly. "She's a nice girl, just not my type."

"Don't be so picky, son. She's an armful of love, and can cook as good as her mom. She's never had a boyfriend either, or so her mom told me."

I wonder why…

"Well, I'll think about coming. I'll see how tired I am by to-morrow night."

"I won't take no for an answer." The mayor thumped him on the shoulder, and Tim winced. "As a matter of fact, if you don't show up, I'll come pick you up myself, with Dolly driving shotgun."

Tim narrowed his eyes, knowing the mans' mischievous character. This was something he just *might* follow through on.

"I'll try and come, like I said. But *please* don't bring Dolly over to my place."

Major Grimley shrugged. "No promises, son. I'm the may-or, you know. Just trying to keep the peace and look after the good citizens under my care. Have to keep the farmers and their wives happy—and especially their daughters, too." His grin was absolutely devilish.

Tim was suspicious now. He was fairly certain that Mrs. Winkle had personally talked to the mayor and asked him for help regarding her daughter's affections. But it was unlike Mayor Grimley to be pushing any girls on Tim. Nudging, yeah…That was pretty common. And he'd always treated Tim like his own son, maybe because he was childless himself, or perhaps due to the tragedy of Tim's family. In return, Tim liked the mayor a lot.

But didn't always agree with his methods… He decided to drop this particular subject.

"Is there a band this year?"

"You bet! Jimmy Blare and the Squares, why who else? They're the only band in town anyway. But a good bunch of guys. Just gotta' keep them sober until the last set." He laughed. "Might have to do the same for myself, son. A drink in hand is good for the blood, they say. I watch what I eat and drink, you know."

Tim felt a comment on the tip of his tongue, but didn't want to rile the mayor up *too* much, or he just might call Dolly over to the town hall this very minute. But the mayor added the jab for him.

"And I do a lot of watching, if you know what I mean." He really bellowed now, and Tim only shook his head at the man's merriment towards his own jokes. Yeah, Mayor Grimley sure owned a great sense of humor—at anyone's expense, including himself. Fair and off-balanced...

"You should have been a comedian. You might have gone far."

"I just might have at that. But I love it here. Wouldn't give up this slot for anything in the world. Besides, they keep voting me in every year. What can I do?"

It was true enough. Mayor Grimley was overwhelmingly popular, and everyone liked the man. Although there was little excitement in the community, the people wanted it that way, and the man was happy to oblige, maintaining tradition at every angle. His feet were firmly planted in the soil of Grainersville, so much so that his toes might have sprouted roots of their own if he happened to stand in the same spot for long enough.

Changing subjects again, Tim turned serious. "Any problems lately because of Halloween?"

The mayor frowned. "A few, actually. Some busted mailboxes, eggs thrown on cars in town, toilet paper wrapped around the tree in front of my office. Pranks, nothing too bad. Have my suspicions, though, and believe me, I'm looking into it. *When* I catch the culprits, they'll be whistling a different tune."

Tim believed him. Friendly and carefree as he was, Mayor

Grimley suffered no nonsense when it came to public behavior and damage to personal property, however innocuous it might seem. More than one youth had been given a customized tour of the town jail by Mayor Grimley and his sheriff. For himself, Tim had never been into any trouble, even while still in school. He gave credit to his parents, with their bright outlook on life and their relentless work ethic. He didn't know of another way to carry on. Others may have gone down a far darker road under the tragic circumstances—he had emerged stronger, growing into a fine, respectable young man.

"I hope you find them soon. I don't like to make accusations, but you're probably thinking the same thing as me." Tim knew exactly who the mayor had referred to.

Instead of replying, Mayor Grimley nodded his head, the glimmer in his eyes overriding any need for words. "Oh well, I have to get working on the decorations, and I'm sure you have plenty to do back home. Miss Lenley and Katie Dougherty are coming by soon. And then the *real* work starts this evening and most of the day tomorrow. I'm expecting a big turnout. I want the whole town to have a good time."

"All right, I'll see you later then." Tim turned to go, satisfied with his placement of the pumpkins.

"And listen, Tim, if you want to help later on, Dolly's going to be here with her mom…"

Without looking, Tim already knew the huge smirk which covered the man's face, and he found little humor in the comment. The sting of Pat's rejection was still fresh, and he hardly would consider himself desperate enough for that kind of rebound.

5

There really was a lot of work at home for Tim. Too much for idle thought, which was a good thing. He stayed outside until darkness swallowed the landscape, feeding his animals, sweeping dirt from the floor of the barn, fixing a loose post from the pasture fence, and throwing a dead pigeon into the weeds. There were a lot of them roosting in the barn's upper hold, and he didn't mind it, being an animal lover. But inevitably, he would find one or two which had died, sometimes from wounds inflicted by other pigeons. *That* bothered him. He felt sorry for these creatures, which for unknown reasons had become outcasts, a threat to another bird, or even the whole flock. Sometimes the most harmless creatures could turn on their fellow species on occasion. Tim didn't know exactly why—perhaps they detected the presence of a disease that humans couldn't sense. It was entirely possible.

He remembered an incident many years ago, when his parents had taken him to an amusement park several counties away. Walking over a stone bridge, they stopped at a feed machine, basically a glass gumball unit filled with field corn, to feed the enormous silver carp that cruised in the waters below. Tim, fascinated by the huge fish, threw pellets down, the kernels smacking onto the surface while the carp sucked them in effortlessly. The fish swam lazily about, nudging the silty bottom for prospective tidbits of food. Tim had smiled and giggled, his parents sitting on a bench talking while the boy enjoyed the moment. He fed the carp for a few minutes, and then heard a loud splashing. Ducks were paddling towards the bridge, and Tim held ready several pieces of corn, ready to throw at them when they came within reach.

But he stopped, his heart skipping a beat, his smile melting away.

Three ducks were chasing another duck, pursuing it as they glided along the cool waters, viciously snapping, even battering it with their bodies, attempting to either drive it away or injure it. They continued until they were out of sight, vanishing beneath the bridge into the darkness. Tim's parents had stood, reaching for his hand and unknowingly pulling him away from the appalling sight. The young boy felt physically ill, and wanted to tell his parents about the horrible event, but his mouth was frozen. He simply couldn't talk. His world was viewed through the eyes of innocence, full of sunshine and fun, everything good. But that day he learned something which would stay with him for years—that the world had an ugly side to it as well as good.

His chest swelled with an intense sense of pity for the hapless creature. He never found out what happened to the duck, but his gut told him the others had killed the bird. It was grossly unfair, and he couldn't erase the image from his mind, as it continued to haunt him for many nights to come. It was a tough thing for a young child to witness and learn, but Tim had grown from the vision. Learned to have compassion for others, whether person or animal, and treat all with respect. And that was part of the reason for his friendship with Pat at school. She had also been an outcast of sorts, not necessarily from external viciousness, but her own self-imposed exile, an internal exodus from socializing with her peers.

Yes, Tim had befriended the quiet girl, and they had connected in some way. And now, facing her rejection, his mood was reflective, and he began to question himself instead of blaming Pat's reasons, whatever they were. It wasn't normal for him, but Tim found himself uncomfortably wading in a bit of his own self-pity and depression.

And it didn't feel very good at all.

There was nothing to be done about it, so he finished his evening chores and stood on the front porch for a minute, staring at the jack-o-lanterns sitting on the steps. He'd ended up carving them a few days ago anyway, keeping to the Halloween tradition. Actually, the dark holiday had never been his favorite. All the talk about spooks and weird things along with dressing up seemed odd to him. He didn't think any harm in celebrating, because it was now an American standard, and people looked for any excuse to have a good time. Why not…

But it dredged up unpleasant memories of his parents. He kept going back to that cold October evening when the accident occurred. It was during the week of Halloween. A teenager then, old enough to stay home by himself because of a cold, and this had saved his life. That was the biggest reason Halloween wasn't his favorite time of the year. He loved the fall, the changing of leaves, harvest time, the cool, brisk evening air, but this one day he could do without. The memory of the tragedy happening around Halloween was permanently fixed in his memory, and there was nothing to be done about it. The mind had a unique and baffling way of relating events with other things, such as sights, sounds, and smells, or in this case a specific time of year. If it had happened on Christmas Eve, then Tim was certain he would have felt the same come December twenty-fifth. But it had not. The end of October left him with a feeling of uneasiness and sorrow. It might never change, and so he needed to make the best of it. Continue on as before, and try not to dwell on the past too much.

He locked the doors, followed around by Perkins and Sammy, his two cats. He kept them inside unlike many other farmers. Cats roaming the barn and fields for mice and stray rodents was certainly a mainstay in rural communities, but he wanted them safe and sound in the house. The road wasn't too far off, and wandering nocturnal scavengers could give them trouble, especially if they were sick. It wasn't really a major concern locally, but Tim was very cautious when it came to his animals, and these two were his buddies.

Yawning, he slumped down onto the sofa, flicking on the TV to catch the next day's weather forecast. Politics and world events were of little concern to him. He just didn't have time to worry about anything else. The house and farm were enough for one young man. Tim propped his feet up on a wooden stool, not bothering to take off his work boots, when he was startled by the phone ringing. The first thing that came to his mind was the Mayor. If he continued to prod him about Dolly anymore, Tim would have to meet him on his own terms somehow. Joking was fine, but that man drove him nuts at times. It might be Tim's turn to play some joke on *him* for once…

"Hello?" He asked tentatively, waiting for the smug laughter.

"Tim? Hi, it's Pat."

Pat? This was totally unexpected, and he felt a mixture of surprise and excitement.

"Oh, yeah. Hi, how are you?"

"All right. I just wanted to apologize for the other day. I didn't mean to sound so rude to you."

"Rude? You weren't rude at all. I understand. It's no big deal." He verged on stammering, as he didn't know what to make of this yet. And he certainly didn't want to sound like a complete idiot, either.

"Well, I think I was. Sorry. It's just..." There was an uncomfortable pause, and Tim's imagination went haywire, thinking the worst. She really did have a boyfriend after all, or the dreaded 'I like you as a friend' was next. That line was the absolute worst for any guy looking to date someone they cared about. The pride-killer for sure. He waited for her response, and felt his mouth go dry.

What is it? What's she trying to tell me? Say something...

"I think I will go to the dance with you."

At first, the words didn't register with him. Not at all. Then they sank in slowly, and he was caught off guard. Had she just said that?

"Tim, are you there?"

"Uh, yeah. That's great news. I mean, it should be a fun time and all. How about I pick you up at around, um, six-thirty? I should be done with my chores around here by then, have to, uh, get some stuff done, and the dance starts at seven I think..."

I think? Think? Stupid! I sound like a goof.

"Oh, all right. I guess I'll see you then. Good night."

Click.

And that was it. Short and sweet.

What a weird change of events. Pat had accepted his offer.

He'd be going with her out on a date. A *real* date. Wow. Wasn't that something? It made him feel kinda' weird, and kinda' good at the same time. Mostly good. Of course mostly good…

A date with Pat.

All of a sudden, his mood brightened considerably. Tim smiled, standing up, his earlier nervousness quickly forgotten. Replaced by a much nicer feeling. Along with a different kind of tension. Much better than rejection though. Yeah, a lot better. He walked over to the window, staring outside.

Halloween was a strange season, where the unexpected occurred. But maybe not always bad. *This* was certainly a positive turn of events. The prospect of being out on a date with Pat would be more than just a wish. It was a reality. He was really going to go out with her now.

Don't be overconfident. Just be yourself. Like you were back in school. It wasn't that long ago.

He prepped himself, wanting to cover his angles. It hadn't been very long ago at all. What, two or three years since graduation? And why in the world had he waited so long to talk to her?

Fear. He nodded to himself. Of rejection, of dating. But he was a little bit older now, and more mature. It shouldn't be a big deal.

He sighed, thinking of how busy tomorrow would be in preparation for his date with Pat. He stared up at the stars, and the moon filling the night, rising over the fields like a silver dollar, watching the earth far below.

Maybe—just maybe—in coming years, Halloween would mean something far better and more special to Tim than it had before.

Things were starting to look up nicely.

Pat hung up the phone, gently placing it on the holder. She stared at it for long moments, her heart a nervous twitter in her chest. She took a deep breath, then slowly exhaled. This was the first step, but a very big one. Huge...What would happen? She mouthed a silent prayer. Let it all be over, she thought. Please.

She lifted herself from the chair and looked cautiously around, like a child who has done something bad and was waiting to see if they were caught. The house brooded around her, silent.

But watchful? She couldn't tell.

Pat walked around, moving a chair here, a vase there, straightening curtains, looking for dust. It was a routine, and she was careful not to act too abruptly, out of pattern. She didn't want to fool herself. It had only been a mental decision and a phone call. And she certainly was able to leave the house. At least for a while.

Then again, she had never really tried running away. She always thought there were limits to her movements, how long she could be away, how far she could go. Subtle reminders had been evident, and these had terrified her. But something recently had changed, and now she was testing the restrictions of her prison, was willing to face the consequences. In a way, she felt relieved. Inactivity had been the norm, resignation the invisible marker upon her brow. Trepidation, the unseen cloak laid over her shoulders, smothering her intentions to break free of the chains.

It was her hope that things were different now. Again, there had been no occurrences in a while. She held onto that little fragment of hope, and it would sustain her tomorrow. Beyond.

And if she was wrong…she was prepared to face the horror once again, the silent battle.

She only prayed that Tim wouldn't be brought into the fray.

6

Halloween.

The dark holiday had arrived, dressed in a mantel of darkness, its breath a bleak wind which blew in from the west, where foothills huddled together like titans whispering black tales among comrades.

The trees rattled their welcome to its inevitable call, shaking even more leaves from skeletal limbs, the gaunt branches trembling like the arms of arthritic old men. The house was surrounded by shapes and shadows. The trunks and bushes could have been nameless phantoms oozing out of the cold ground from burial crypts. The moon was bloated, full in its monthly cycle, dressed brilliantly in icy silver. A coin of great beauty, sinister in its own mocking fashion when viewed on such a night.

It was only a handful of minutes past midnight, and the morning would not be nudged awake for a while. Animals slept dreamlessly outside in barn and stable, their masters comfortably inside, warm and secure in their beds. Frost laced windows, leaves scampered beneath fence and under sheds, scratched against asphalt, scuttled like startled crabs in the growing breeze.

There were two nights for this particular day. The first was here. Midnight had now been breached, the clock hands quietly moving past the witching hour and ushering in the true dead of night. But morning had nothing to do with this period of time, where the wings of nightmare held reign, and sleepers shuddered when they passed close overhead.

The world welcomed Halloween, although no witches flew across the moon on dark broomsticks to herald its coming. Restless shades did not rise from lonely graves. Imps didn't prance on brown lawns, scarecrows did not wrest themselves down from wooden gallows.

But goblins *did* indeed walk the earth…

Two figures melted from the gloom, creeping forward along the lawn and closing in on the murky structure. The taller form pointed to the other, and they hunched low to the ground, shuffling along until they reached the porch and moved to the left side of the building. Here, clumps of bushes formed a buffer between the house and grass. Well-clipped, they were broad, of medium height, and offered concealment for the pair.

"It's this side." Joe Harper's voice broke the cold stillness, and his companion stared upwards to the second floor. "That's definitely her window. I've seen her already." There was enough smugness in his tone that left no doubt as to what Joe *really* meant, thought Sam, who rubbed his hands together against the brisk air.

"Uh-huh." Sam whispered his reply, looking around in excitement.

"Now, let's try the window. With any luck, it'll be open."

But there was no luck in their effort to pry the panel outward. It was the type that opened at an angle, with a latch on the inside to secure it. Joe struggled for a few moments, adjusting his gloves, then stepped back. "Well that just sucks…Let me see something."

The frame was old and rotting from long years and moisture. Joe pushed on it with his boot, and they heard the crack of splintering wood. They both worked at it until a section broke off, and Joe went down on hands and knees, moving it loose. After another minute or two, he managed to maneuver the window around, and it steadily gave way. Soon, it was ripped out, exposing an interior of darkness and shadows.

"I'll go first. Keep quiet."

Joe took a flashlight from his pocket, pointing it inside before descending. The window was several feet off the basement floor, and he dropped down without difficulty. He then waited for his stockier companion, and Sam followed, huffing and scraping his way in, his bulkier frame barely allowing him entrance.

"Quiet…" Joe smacked him on the head with the flashlight, causing the other to wince in pain.

"She's asleep by now," Sam offered in defense, but Joe would have nothing to do with the excuse.

"You don't know that for sure. Not another word until I say so, or else you're going back outside."

Sam nodded sheepishly, but his eyes gleamed with excitement. Joe noticed the eagerness in his friend's expression, and wondered if he looked the same. He probably did, but he could care less. He splashed the basement with his beam, the light adequate enough to reveal the dim surroundings.

It appeared as if Pat had no use for this area. Old furniture, chairs and a pair of tables, were pushed against the far wall. They spotted a dresser, several closed storage boxes, a wash line with clothes hanging on it, and an assortment of other discarded, or unwanted items. The wooden stairs loomed in the background, and Joe headed towards them. Their boots sounded dull against the stone flooring, and Joe reached the bottom stair. He put a finger against his lips, pivoting to his friend, but Sam was already staring upwards, a cruel smile beginning to form.

For the first time, Joe hesitated, questioning their actions. He'd never done anything like this before. Broken into a few barns, the town store once, sure. But all of them empty places—the owners gone, or occupied elsewhere. This was totally different. Pat was certainly in the house, and she was the target of their intrusion. And their presence had nothing to do with burglary, or juvenile pranks...the consequences of being caught were severe, and they couldn't afford to screw up. Especially Sam, who was pretty much a bumbling idiot. He also happened to be Joe's only real friend.

And *Sam* had certainly never conceived of doing something this terrible.

Joe's moment of indecision melted away. The stakes were high, and it gave him an incredible rush of adrenalin. He took the first step up the stairs, and the rest were easier now. Much easier...

They reached the top, pausing.

For a second, Joe's heart skipped a beat. Had he heard something?

He turned around to look at Sam, who waited there, startled by his friend's reaction. Joe mouthed the word 'hear' and pointed to his own ears, but his companion shook his head. Joe flashed the beam behind them, searching for any indication of movement. He would have sworn that he heard something—a creaking, as of wood being split apart. The sound had clearly come from the basement, behind them somewhere in the dark. He continued waiting, for well over a minute. There was no room for mistakes.

But nothing materialized. It *was* an old house, after all. Structures settled, pipes made noise, mice scurried about, and a million other things could be responsible. Satisfied that it was nothing, he reached for the door handle, twisting it slowly. To his anger, it wouldn't turn.

Locked!

Damn, now why would she lock the cellar door? She didn't even use the place. He hadn't expected to find it locked, and he paused, more uncertain than ever now. Joe was confident that he could pick the lock, but he didn't have a screwdriver or other tool with him. Stupid, he thought. Neither himself or Sam— *especially* Sam—had foreseen any problems breaking into the old place and gaining quick access. They'd been too sure of themselves.

Behind him, Sam held up his arms in frustration. Joe shook his head, thinking. He could break it by force, but that was taking a serious risk. If Pat happened to be up, she would know immediately that someone had broken inside, and she'd call the police. That was not a risk worth taking.

Joe turned, motioning for Sam to go back downstairs. His friend reluctantly obeyed, and they were on the basement floor in seconds, descending quietly. Joe pushed Sam back to the window, where he felt safer to talk.

"Not now. We'll come back later with some tools. I can't take the chance of waking her up by breaking the lock." His voice was laced with disappointment and anger, and he shot Sam a withering look, daring him to contradict his plan, and his failure to be prepared.

The other youth frowned. "Don't you have anything in the car?"

"No, you idiot. Would I have just told you that? I left my tool pouch back in my dad's garage when I was working on the stereo yesterday. We'll come back. Tomorrow, or tonight. Whatever it is."

Sam was silent, looking around warily. "This place gives me the creeps. She lives here all alone, with all this junk down here, locked away. Weird, man."

"I told you she's weird. Who do you think killed her aunt and uncle?"

"But they never found anything. You really think she killed them, hid the bodies, and fooled everyone?"

Joe replied without hesitation. "Yeah, I do. I think she's one smart, twisted girl. She got away with murder."

"Hey, maybe the bodies are buried down here somewhere."

Sam's remark seemed stupid, as usual, but standing there in the gloom, inside the actual *place* for the first time, sent real chills scurrying up Joe's spine. He'd been quick to condemn Pat for her alleged atrocities in his own warped conscience, but mainly as a cover for the despicable act *he* was ready to do. Now, he wondered if Sam's comment contained any measure of truth. What if the bodies *were* hidden somewhere? The basement would be a likely spot. But it didn't make any sense. The police had certainly scoured the building when the pair vanished. They couldn't have been that incompetent to have missed the obvious. Could they?

He didn't believe that. For the most part, at least.

"Let's look around before we leave." Sam's brashness was annoying, mainly because *he* was sounding like the risk taker now, while Joe appeared to be the cautious one.

It pissed Joe off, too.

"Just for a minute. I'll shine the light on the floor. Look for any cracks, or something that don't look right."

They moved around, checking the floor for anything out of place. The ground was a typical basement for older homes in the area, with concrete as foundation. It was hard to imagine Pat could have dug up a spot and covered it over, fooling everyone, especially several years ago as a teenager. Pretty crazy. But then again, he'd heard stranger things. The two of them searched around for a few minutes, fingering cracks, kneeling down, looking for any sign to back up Sam's wild claim. Besides dust and small, broken chunks of aging concrete, they came up empty. Joe then noticed another door at ground level, way in the back of the basement.. From the looks, it was an old cold cellar, most likely once used to store canned fruits and vegetables.

"What do you think's in there?" Joe outlined the faded panel, which once had been painted blue, but now was chipped and flaking. A metal latch handle was closed, and Joe tried it, finding it locked.

"What's behind door number one?"

Joe tested it, not as worried about the noise carrying from this isolated part of the house. The lock was rusty, and he banged on it lightly with the casing from his flashlight. It gave quickly, and he nodded, slowly opening it. Sam looked behind them, towards the stairs, but the house was deathly silent. Joe craned his neck inside, unwilling to entirely trust his luck. Maybe she had set a trap or something. An alarm even? He was tempted to push Sam first, but thought better of it. A smarter plan was to check things out himself, not let his companion blow it for the both of them. He inched his head further inside. The room was tight, damp and empty. Disappointed, Joe grumbled in disgust. Sam moved alongside him now.

"Hey, shine the light over there." Sam pointed to the far corner, while Joe frowned, seeing nothing. "On the ground. Looks like a hole or something."

Joe *did* see it now…There was an opening in the floor. Cautiously he approached, Sam in tow. Leaning over, he peered downwards through a round hole, his light reflecting off something several dozen yards below. Water. It was a well. And that fact pointed to a chilling possibility about the suspect events which had taken place in the house a few years back.

"Damn. Maybe you're right, Joe. She killed them, and threw the bodies down there. Wow."

Staring down the gaping black maw of the well, Joe now wondered himself. Had he been right with his far-fetched theory? He wasn't kidding himself that it was a fabrication to excuse what they meant to do to her, but then again, if she was bad enough to kill her own family and get away with it, well, she deserved what she had coming to her then. Joe felt some justification, in his own twisted mind.

"You know, I just thought of something else." Sam scratched his head, the piggish eyes wide and staring.

"Well, what is it?" Joe was impatient. Things were not going as anticipated, and he was ready to gather his losses for another day..

"Maybe she's dangerous."

At first, the statement sounded ridiculous, but then, down there in the darkness, it appeared to have possibilities of a much more sinister nature. Joe swallowed, his spine crawling with chills.

"We better be careful with her, Joe."

But Joe had no intention of being careful with the girl. Sam was really beginning to bother him now. Maybe she did away with her aunt and uncle, but Pat certainly would be no match for these two, prepared and pretty dangerous themselves. No way.

It was time for them to leave. The moment was past, and he didn't trust to luck much longer. There was plenty of time for them, no rush. Finding the well was interesting, maybe important, maybe not...Definitely had no bearing on their own plans though. And there was a decent chance they would find out the real truth soon, Joe thought, the smirk on his face hellish.

"Let's go. She'll never find out we were down here. Looks like she hasn't been in the basement for a few years. Pat's been a naughty girl, with a guilty conscience, I think. C'mon, out."

Sam remained leaning over the rim, fascinated by what it could mean. Joe spun his light across the floor in a final sweep, and Sam gasped.

"What? What's wrong?"

Sam didn't answer, but backed away as quickly as he could considering his clumsiness. "Something down there. I swear I saw something down there…"

"Like what? You're seeing things." At least Joe *hoped* he was.

Fearfully, he pointed the flashlight into the murky depths. After several long moments, he spat in disgust. "Nothing, you idiot. What are you talking about?"

Sam crept forward. "I don't know. The wall moved, or something."

"Are you nuts? How can a wall move? Are you on crack?"

Uncertain now, Sam shook his head. "I don't know, but it looked weird. Like it was bending or something."

"That's crazy. And so are you. You're imagining things now." Sam peered down the opening. Then Joe continued, edging him on. "Plus you're in the house of a killer. I think you're just scared."

"No I'm not…"

"Yeah, well *I* think you are. I might have to come here alone. Now let's *go*."

This time he shoved Sam so hard he almost fell into the well. Joe grabbed his arm at the last second, laughing evilly. He pushed him towards the door, giving him an extra shove to the rump with his boot. Closing the door behind him, Joe gave the basement the once over with his flashlight, almost forgetting where they were and more importantly *why*...

They hurried over to the window, Sam going first, boosted by Joe, and then the taller youth after. They replaced the window, fixing it best they could, until Joe was convinced it wouldn't look suspicious unless someone knelt down before it. He glanced up at the dark bedroom window, shuddering involuntarily as he imagined invisible eyes peering down on him.

They hurried across the lawn, ducking between cover, and left.

Tim was up early, greeting Halloween with a mixture of conflicting emotions. Memories of his parents trailed after him like unseen spirits while he dressed and ate breakfast. He honored them through thought and a silent prayer, pressing his fingers to his lips when he looked down at the picture on the living room table which pictured them both with huge smiles, sitting side by side on a pair of chestnut colored horses. He felt a tear on his cheek, and he gently brushed it away.

"Guys, I think things are gonna' be different this year. I might have found someone else, lonely like me. Don't know if you ever seen her, maybe you did. Pat's her name. Nice, quiet girl. She lost her family just like I did."

He reflected for a few moments, trying to clear his head. Things were hazy before him. The date with Pat tonight at the harvest dance, just the fact that she'd said yes after first saying no was still hard to swallow. It suddenly occurred to him that she still could refuse. That would really hurt. Dashing his hopes after the emotional ups and downs. Then again, it wouldn't be the end of the world. His parents were gone, and he'd survived.

The sun rose each day, and he carried on with his work. A lot of it stemmed from his resoluteness in keeping the farm. Another season or two and he would be working all the fields, and not have to lease out any. He was getting close, and had a handle on things. He could operate all the equipment, and also fix much of it as well. Tim had learned tons, and every passing day was a new lesson for him.

But it was Halloween again, and despite his feelings and memories, the past existed, couldn't be erased. He respected this, embraced it fully, but kept his head arched skyward, hoping for a more fortunate future. He managed a small smile, thinking of Pat, and how his parents might react to his asking her out. He was sure they would have liked her a lot. His hesitation had been a mistake. Now was the chance to make up for lost time. He returned to his bedroom, searching about in the closet for what he would wear tonight. It struck him then that he'd never asked Pat about a costume. Not everyone wore one, maybe half of the people, if that. It bothered him that he'd overlooked this matter, and he sat down on the bed, wondering if she wanted to dress up.

Should I call her up and ask?

Tim was reluctant to do so. He wasn't superstitious as such, but still, the thought of jinxing his date was unnerving. Well, he would have something ready just in case. There were some old masks in the basement from his childhood trick-or-treating days, and he would take a couple with him tonight as a backup plan. Yeah. Good idea.

With that settled, Tim hurried downstairs and laced his work boots. Pulling on a flannel shirt and jacket, he dipped his head outside for a second to check on the weather. It was cloudy, windy, and the air had a nasty bite to it. The forecast was right on, and the temperature would not break the forty-five degree mark today. Tonight, unseasonably cold. All in all, a rather gloomy All Hallow's Eve, the atmosphere doing its best to bring an appropriate witches' brew of moody and drab weather to celebrate the darkest holiday. The wind rushed past Tim's face, scattering the fallen leaves around the oak and acorn trees which fronted the house, making it look like a lane straight out of Washington Irving's *The Legend of Sleepy Hollow*. He remembered his early-grade teachers reading to him about Ichabod Crane and his ill-fated encounter with the Headless Horseman. One of his classmates had made fun of the name, pronouncing it *Itch-a-bod*, which made Tim angry. But that's what kids tended to do. Anything which struck them as being the slightest bit unusual was considered fair game. Person, place or thing. No exceptions. Tim's line of thinking was different though… He'd always supported the underdog—the poor, scarecrow-thin schoolmaster, who found himself at odds with the brawny, formidable character of Brom Bones. The tale was masterfully written, one which left you wondering about the ending. Had Ichabod really met his demise at the hands of the frightful specter, or was it actually his earthly rival, dressed in sinister and convincing disguise? And were the rumors mentioned at the end of the story true? Had the schoolmaster been spirited away, or had he relocated, moving away to take up a new position in a different town?

Tim liked to think it was the latter possibility. He *much* preferred happy endings in stories. All stories…Real or not.

He snapped his head back inside the house, debating on whether to put on a thicker jacket or not. His thoughts drifted back to the dance tonight, and his date. What a mixture of strange notions going through his head this early on Halloween.

Memories of his parents, Sleepy Hollow, the harvest dance,

and Pat.

Should prove to be quite an interesting day, he thought. Yes, indeed.

Pat slept late.

Her sleep had been disturbed by nightmares, the memories of which had been forever erased in that period of time which nestled between slumber and a measure of alertness, a corridor of liquid imagination, where reality and fantasy intersected, blurred, and separated, either to be lost in black oblivion, or absorbed by the infinite halls of the mind and sealed within. Pat remembered times when she'd had such beautiful, pleasurable dreams. Upon waking, she was in the middle of some action. Sometimes it was as simple as a stroll along a woodland stream, the sun blinking mischievously through the forest canopy. Others were more fantastic, like flying unfettered through the air, relishing the magnificence of freedom, wild and reckless. She understood that these fantasies reflected her worldly prison, and within these dreams she fought against her shackles and those who watched her. She didn't recall what disturbed her this past night, but the *source* was obvious. Her reality produced ample fodder for the most dreadful of nightmares.

Pat glanced around her bedroom, looking for signs of activity.

Things appeared normal, and lately, she was less reluctant to worry about focusing on the house and its hidden keepers, which may or may not still exist. Pat tested, probed, in subtle ways, insignificant in any other situation familiar to any other person. But she was not like anyone else, and her life had been as far removed from normal as could be imagined.

She sat up on the edge of her bed.

Curtains drawn, it was dim inside the small room, which might have been considered cozy in the proper context. The lamp was lit, as she always kept it. Total darkness was an abomination to her. If light had been restricted, taken away, she surely would have lost her mind years ago. Light, to Pat, represented hope, however tiny a fragment it appeared. Darkness was the great monster, concealing the blackest secrets of the universe. Things lay hidden in such a consuming cloak. Terrible things.

Pat stood, pulling a robe around her slender shoulders. At times she felt so old, like she had lived in the house for a hundred years. It was a future she wanted no part of. Better to end it all long before. One way or the other...

She yawned, moving to the window and looking outside at the autumn landscape. Wind, leaves, frost on the pumpkin. On October's heels, the day was here, one which would be pivotal to the course of her life as it had been these past several years. The wind vane on the barn twirled about, teased by the breeze. Back and forth, back and forth...Directionless, uncertain of where to point next. Just like her. Yes. They were the same thing. What did fate have in store for them both?

Pat felt nervous, fearful, hopeful. A blend of emotions spilled from her troubled heart. Had it all come to this, right now? Her mind was rife with chaos. It seemed fitting that it was the last day of October.

Halloween had certainly arrived.

Pivoting, she stared harshly at the walls of her home. Her prison. *Daring* something to materialize, at the same time voicing a silent prayer that nothing would happen, and things were normal again. What a strange word. Normal...What did it even mean to her? She walked right up to the wall and stopped.

"Well, if you're here come out. I'm tired of being a prisoner, being watched. I'm done. If you still exist, do your best now. You're not going to keep me anymore. Go back to wherever you came from!"

She screamed the last words, and the dam inside her finally burst. Tears welled down her cheeks, and she pounded against the walls, slumping down until her fists hurt. Pat knelt there for several minutes, realizing that her barrier of inaction had lifted, the fear of retribution gone. It was done at last.

She would accept the consequences...if there was anything yet to accept.

Rubbing her eyes dry, she looked up, her gaze sweeping the room. Nothing moved. The walls were silent, the house brooding around her. In the past, such action would have initiated activity. It would have happened quickly, terrifying her. But now, the home seemed dead, except for herself.

Dead. That was another appropriate word for the day. Everyone had their 'dead.' Loved ones who were gone from the world. Pat's family was among them—her Aunt Trish, whom she adored, despite the woman's relentless teasing. And her Uncle Ray and Aunt Margie, the pair raising her from infancy, her real mother dying in childbirth, her husband killed when his tractor plowed over a hidden ditch, throwing him helplessly through the windshield.

Regrets. Pat kept her dead near, thinking of them always. Talking to them in her mind over the years, asking them for help.

And for forgiveness.

She swallowed, her throat thick. It was the *one* thought which plagued her the past several years, and a terrible one at that. She could face the nightmare of her life, even the faceless keepers which lived in the house. Withstand the utter horror, despite not understanding its nature or purpose. But the one thing which bothered her beyond all these things, was a question which might never have a clear answer.

What if *she* had caused the deaths of her family?

It was time.

Tim sat in his pickup, flicking on the small light switch in the mirror and checking out his hair. It looked fine. Opened his mouth, looked at his teeth. Yeah, nothing going on in there, although he felt the slightest tingle far in the back, thinking he'd either scrubbed too hard or a cavity was in its earliest stages. Something to worry about another day. Definitely not now.

He opened the door, stepping out into the night. Greeted by the full moon, he shivered. The night felt different some-how. Magical. Halloween *was* unique, and not just because of his own personal feelings. There was something else about it as well. True, there were all the tales of spirits walking the earth, goblins and witches and other stuff. Of course he didn't believe in any of that, not even ghosts. If he ever saw one for real, that would change things. Until then, forget it.

The history and legends behind the holiday were probably the reason people felt the difference on this night, truth be told. But also, there was some real magic going on right now. His date with Pat. He felt a bit weird. Not starry-eyed, or anything like that. Just, well…he tried to find the proper words. Touched? A little romantic. He liked to think this was another type of magic. *Good* magic.

Blushing schoolboy again…

Man, he hated feeling so foolish. But it was also pretty cool in a way.

He walked up to the porch, where the pumpkins had transformed into grinning jack-o-lanterns. Carved by the hands of an expert, he thought. She had a knack for it. His own pumpkins looked amateurish in comparison, but kids never trick-or-treated to his house anyway. There were few neighbors, all of them farmers. They preferred going to the dance as a celebration, but it was more a big social event where the hard working farmers of the community talked about the harvest, exchanging stories, complaints, and predictions. Some of the outlying folk took their children into town, where several businesses put out fruit drinks and candy for any of the young costumed visitors, and the mayor always had a table inside his own office heaped with sugary snacks. Of course, Mayor Grimley's hands were constantly picking at the treats as well. He claimed to be testing for razor blades, despite the fact that he bought all the candy himself…No one believed him.

Tim knocked on the door, listening as the sound fell dead in the cool air. He waited for a few moments, whistling to himself. Anxious. He needed to remember not to look nervous tonight, no matter what. Stay relaxed, have fun. Like they were back in school. It seemed natural that the two of them would get together, considering their backgrounds, and current social lives. Poor Pat probably never went anywhere. She really needed to get out of the house more.

He looked the home over with greater detail as he waited

there. The place *looked* lonely. Sitting between large fields, the house was old, your typical country home, exposed to the wind, as there were few trees, and not much else. Bushes, a long fence. The place wasn't falling apart, but it had an uneasy feel about it. This bothered Tim, although he didn't want to think anything negative concerning Pat, or things associated with her. He certainly wouldn't mention it. That was a disaster in the making. But the home didn't have that cozy, warm exterior which welcomed an embrace, a trait many houses in the country possessed. He shook his head. Why let such stupid notions distract him? The pressure of the forthcoming date? But he didn't think that was the reason.

If he didn't know any better, he would have thought there were some bad vibes here. But Tim wouldn't go there. He had no special psychic gifts, and gave little or no heed to such things.

He was just *nervous* right now. That was all.

The door opened, and Pat stood in the frame, wearing a plain, green dress, a light from the living room casting her face in shadow. Tim smiled, and gave a little wave with his hand, more a physical effort to boost his own self-confidence than anything else.

"Hello, Tim."

"Hi. You look great. All ready?"

She hesitated in the doorway for a moment, pausing in the middle of her movement. Tim felt awkward, and really had nothing to say right now. The pleasantries were brief, and he desperately hoped they both would open up as the night went on. For now, he had to be polite and attentive. But not too mechanical.

Pat stepped through, then closed the door behind her, locking it fast. She stared at the wooden frame for just a second, but long enough to make Tim wonder if she was looking for something.

"All right, I'm ready." She took a deep breath, and her voice contained the slightest quiver.

Is she as nervous as I am?

"Got my pickup truck here, but don't worry, there's plenty of room. She rides nice."

Pat nodded, but didn't respond.

Have to be more interesting than that. Dumb. What does she care about a truck…

He gave himself a mental kick in the ass. They walked to his vehicle, Tim remembering to open the door for her. She looked him in the eyes, and the ghost of a smile appeared. Tim was no expert, but it appeared genuine, and that made him feel really good.

He smiled back, full and genuine.

"Happy Halloween," he said. And maybe it would finally be a *good* one. There was hope for him. And just maybe, the both of them.

"Happy Halloween," Pat replied quietly.

They left, Tim turning the truck around and heading for town.

"Well isn't that just sweet." Joe folded his arms as he crouched down, concealed in the field across from the house, watching the pair drive off.

"With Tim yet. I don't believe it." Sam huffed, pulling the knit hat over his ears.

"He's dating the town killer. Timmy better be careful," Joe said, his tone mocking, but he was unable to disguise his jealousy.

"Now what? I wonder where they're going?"

"The dance, you idiot. Where else would they be going in this stinking little craphole of a town, on Halloween yet?"

Sam straightened, then nodded. "Yeah, you're right. The harvest dance. My sister's going too, with Becky Grable."

"She's a lesbian."

"No she's not."

"I mean your sister."

"You're just pissed she doesn't like you."

Joe spat. "Couldn't care less about that cow."

"Well, what are we going to do?"

"We'll wait." Joe left the cover of the high cornstalks, frowning as the wind smacked against his face.

"Not here, I hope."

"No. Inside the house." Joe brought out his tool pouch. "Let's go trick-or-treating. The *real* treat will be later..."

The two crossed the road, heading for the side of the building.

Tim and Pat walked up to the entrance of the town hall, where a bonfire was crackling merrily, the smell of burning wood drifting about the parking lot. Firefly sparks showered the air, and a number of giggling children huddled about the welcoming blaze with marshmallow sticks beneath the supervision of two women, who Tim recognized as Marie Hanesfolt and Barb Ellen.

Helen Ringhold peeked around the half-open door, eyeing the plate of marshmallows. "Save me one!" She squeaked. "Or I won't let you back in."

"Do you believe that threat?" Barb nudged her companion, who was too busy examining toasted puffs to care. "Get back to work, Helen. Here's a nice pair of youngsters waiting to get in. Why, I think that's Tim Burker there. Hi Tim. Who's the lucky lady?"

Tim waved, handing his tickets to Helen. "This is Pat Kuch-er."

At the name, all three women stared over at her. Tim swallowed, feeling another uncomfortable moment coming on, but to his immense relief it passed quickly, the ladies all smiling and telling her how glad they were she'd decided to come.

"…so happy to see you."

"Wonderful. How are you, my dear?"

"Pat, you've grown since I seen you last. Quite the lovely young lady now. Make sure Tim doesn't step on your toes on the dance floor…"

Pat nodded politely. Tim couldn't tell who said what, but it was obvious that the girl's appearance was a pleasant surprise to these women as they tried to make her feel at home. A few seconds later (and more than one remark to make sure they ate their fill), the two were inside the building, immediately part of the milling throng which moved about in all directions.

Tim motioned for her to follow, and he picked out two seats at the end of a long table near the far wall. A band was playing on the stage, the musicians all dressed like skeletons, which was a neat touch. A fiddler was soloing to Charlie Daniel's *The Devil Went Down to Georgia*, and the wooden floor was filled with a mixture of couples square dancing, some *trying* to square dance, and others moving their arms and legs about in some semblance of moving to the beat, failing badly. Small children scampered about in the corners in their own ragtag imitations, a few of them doing no worse than some of the adults.

"Farmers can't dance too well." Tim tried his hand at humor, and to his surprise, Pat gave him a small smile. She looked really cute, now that Tim could sit face-to-face with her. His palms felt sweaty, and his back itched, but that couldn't be helped. A few heads turned their way, but no one approached.

The turnout was excellent, and about half of the people wore costumes. The usual October suspects were all out tonight. There walked an unscary ghost, the material apparently swiped from some poor farmer's tattered bed sheet. Here sat a scarecrow, stiff in burlap and drinking a glass of beer. Not a crow in sight…Holding hands and prancing ridiculously in front of the stage were a trio of witches, looking suspiciously like the Gensemer sisters, who could always be counted on as being the life of the party, if not through their off-color humor, then by their late-night drunken antics. And it was still pretty early yet…Tim pointed them out to Pat, who seemed amused by his description.

Decorations covered the building. Tablecloths were spread out, all of them matching in the traditional orange and black markings. Glasses with orange votives were placed on every table, each one of them filled to the brim with candy corn. On the rafters overhead, someone had taken the time to hang a monstrous purple bat which swayed dreamily, several orange balloons joining it against the ceiling. Tim's own pumpkins were sprawled against the wall, along with many others including some massive Cinderella varieties, dozens of gourds and jack-be-littles, two stuffed scarecrows, and tall cornstalks everywhere. There were plenty of *these* to go around… In one corner, children were already lining up for the annual apple bobbing contest, to be immediately followed by the adult version, which always proved to be a raucous event.

"Last year Ben Hawkins won. He accidentally swallowed a mouthful and was choking like a fish out of water," Tim explained. "He panicked and chipped one of his front teeth on the rim of the barrel."

Pat giggled, and it was a pleasant sound, bringing a soft smile to Tim's face.

"You need a drink? I'll grab us two. Soda, or apple cider? Or a beer?" He smirked. "I really don't drink myself, one or two a year."

"Hold off on the beer, but the apple cider sounds good, especially if it's hot."

"Be right back." Tim stood, then hesitated for a moment. "I forgot to thank you."

"For what?"

"Well, for being here, coming out with me, Pat."

The girl paused, her face growing serious. "It's *you* who needs to thanked. You never forgot about me. And Tim, I've thought about you as well. I've been so lonely, you can't imagine..."

Her voice grew husky, and now it was Tim's turn to feel emotional. He moved over, and squeezed her hand. "It's all right. I figure we have a lot in common. It's been hard—real hard—managing on my own. We're both orphans, in a way. But we survived. I can see how you're hurting, but you'll be fine. You're strong."

Tim fidgeted, then took a small wrapped package from his pocket. "For you, just a little something. You can open it later on."

Pat couldn't find words. She sat there, taking the tiny box in her hand, pressing it against her heart. "Thank you," she finally whispered. "You didn't have to..."

He held up one hand. "Later. But now, the drinks." Tim turned, almost bumping into a hobo holding a pitcher of beer. "Whoa..." He raised his hands in the air, apologizing. With a last grin to her, he went up to the bar, disappearing into the crowd.

How *kind* he was being to her, she thought. She swallowed with affection. Tim hadn't changed one bit. In school, he was always friendly and warm, willing to overlook her shyness and accept her for who she was. She cared for him, and had thought about him a lot after graduation. And unknown to him, had watched him ride past her house on many occasions, hoping for some connection. For her, Tim had opened the door again to the outside world. The question remained though, if she would be permitted access to it, and for how long.

Pat just sat there, absorbing her surroundings.

It was so wonderful spending time with Tim, and interacting with people again. How she had *missed* this. Such simple pleasures denied to her. She didn't need to see and travel the world—although it would be fun some day—but just have the experience of daily freedom. To come and go as she pleased. Not worry about what an extended stay away from home might bring about. Pat had rebelled now, taken a huge first step, and had no regrets. She had fought, refusing to remain a voiceless prisoner who'd been incarcerated for reasons beyond her understanding. That was over... At least, her willing compliance. Right now, she wasn't sure what anything meant. The house had been dormant for a while, failing to react to her recent outburst of emotion and attention. She prayed it was finished, and clung to this hope desperately, but understood that she might very well be wrong. And if anything *did* happen, she would make damn sure that Tim wouldn't be involved more than he was already. He would be terribly hurt by her pushing him away, but it would be for his own safety. And he'd given her a gift now…Several gifts tonight. She cared about him greatly. Tim. He was honest, good-natured, with a heart of gold. Also, as he proclaimed, a survivor of family tragedy. Just like her. On the surface they had much in common.

If one dug deeper, however, they were as different as night and day.

They were filled with malice, two outsiders in the community who could care less about anything which didn't benefit their own desires, and were takers, relishing at the cost of others. They were young yet, and had just begun to push the barriers within themselves and the tolerance of those around them. Joe was clever in some ways, but not as much as he'd liked to think. Tall and strong, he pushed his way around in high school, picking on the smaller kids, the typical bully. His antics had stopped short though when someone bigger than himself had pinned him against a wall in the locker room, humiliating him in front of his classmates. Since then, it had been all downhill for Joe, the scar of embarrassment never healing since that day. And in any way that he could, the whole world would be made to pay the price. Eventually, little by little. This *was* a small community, after all. He was just beginning.

Sam was born to be a follower, and tended to more wicked pursuits for recreation. He liked to *hurt* things. Animal, bug, plant. It didn't really matter. Once he might have had a conscience, but watching his alcoholic father drink his life away in bars and at home, paying the bills by government disability checks and selling dope on the side, did nothing but further Sam's eroding sense of decency or purpose over the years.

The youths slipped into the basement window, their minds filled with accumulated trash and resentment. They were not the smartest criminals, but they did have much in common. Hatred, jealousy, lust. In no particular order...Whatever opportunity arose.

And tonight it was Pat. Lonely, weird, cute. A perfect blend for the two misfits and their nasty plans.

They rummaged around the cellar, taking their time. They knew where Pat was, and she wouldn't be returning for a while. An hour or two, they decided. And she would find them waiting for her.

"All this junk. Worthless crap." Sam kicked an old chair, breaking its leg as he laughed.

"Hey, make sure not to take those gloves off and leave fingerprints. Unless you want to get caught."

Sam held up his hands. "These aren't going anywhere."

"Better not screw this up. And I hope your dad stays dead drunk. He's our alibi in case anyone comes looking. We were at your house all night. Nobody can prove it one way or the other with your sister gone."

"Don't worry." Sam rooted through the carton, searching for anything of interest.

"What's in that one?" Both of them pointed their flashlights inside, illuminating the contents. They found dusty glassware, toys a child might play with, and several framed pictures.

"Look. This must have been her family." Joe tapped the back of it. The photograph showed Pat, maybe twelve or thirteen at the time, with two adults. All three of them were standing in front of the barn in the backyard. There was nothing special about it. Her aunt and uncle had their hands placed over Pat's shoulders, and her eyes looked dull, her face expressionless.

Joe ignored it, while Sam reached over for a look himself. "*That's* weird."

"What?" Joe moved on to something else, his voice expressing little interest.

"This picture."

"Yeah, what about it? No big deal. Pat and her family, aunt and uncle, I guess."

"Did you notice something in the corner though? Talk about creepy, man."

Now Joe turned towards him, snatching the frame. "Where? I don't know what you're talking about."

Sam pointed to the spot, and Joe stared hard at it now, leaning close. His eyes narrowed, and he opened his mouth in surprise. "What is it?"

"I don't know, but it freaks me out. Did someone mess around with the picture, maybe?" Sam whispered.

They both examined it more closely now. Against the barn was an anomaly of some type. A swelling in the wood, as if it were made of liquid, or flexible material. And within the bulge were a pair of indistinct objects, which could almost pass for hands. Almost…They were silent for several moments, trying to figure out what it was they were looking at. Sam brought out more items, including additional pictures. There were only a few, but what they found was unnerving. Pat was shown in each one, some by herself, others with her aunt or uncle. And every single photo had something peculiar about it. A blur here, a marking there. Nothing as strange as the first, but weird enough as a coincidence.

"Maybe these are all bad pictures, and they kept them to-gether." Joe shrugged.

"I don't know." Sam was reluctant to agree. "Maybe, but it's still pretty weird."

"C'mon, let's check the upstairs. I don't want to waste time down here anymore. I want to get that door open. And then we'll see what she has up there."

They headed for the stairs, Joe with tool pouch in hand. The lock was rusted, and to Joe's dismay, it wouldn't give at first. Frustrated, he took out a hammer, smashing the lock angrily. The sound carried throughout the basement, and Sam looked back several times over his shoulder. It finally broke open after one last severe pounding, which made Sam cringe. The echoes carried eerily along the walls as if they were in a small audito-rium, and not an old country home.

They looked at each other, and then Joe opened the door. They were in the small kitchen, a tidy place with everything in perfect order, counters impeccable. A wooden table sat in the middle with a single chair. Sam went to the refrigerator, sniffing. "Wonder what she has in here to eat..."

Joe, agitated, snapped at him. "Check the place out first. There's something strange about her. She's whacked out."

Sam looked inside, finding nothing of real interest. Fruits, bread, milk and vegetables. "Skinny bitch," he mumbled.

They moved into the dining room next, which held a larger table in the middle, a corner shelf, candle sconces, and an as-sortment of handmade fixtures. "Doesn't look like the home of a killer." Sam picked up a dinner plate as if he'd never seen one before.

"You know, I just thought of something...Maybe we should cover our tracks better." Joe placed both hands on his hips, nodding to himself and looking pleased.

"What do you mean?"

"Well, after we're done with her, the original plan was to take off. Keep our masks on and she'll never recognize us anyway. But that might not be enough. It's a big chance we're taking. We're talking about the rest of our lives if we get caught." Joe stared over at Sam, whose face was empty of any expression.

"I guess so. Wait a second. Are you talking about *killing* her?"

Joe never hesitated, his eyes fixed on his companion, daring to contradict him. "Yeah."

"You never said anything about that..." Sam looked at him, the piggish eyes blinking madly, a normal reaction for him when he was really nervous.

"I told you—I'm *not* messing around here. We're doing something new, so the risk is a lot bigger. If you can't hang with it, then get the hell out right now."

Sam looked down at his feet, shuffled about, wiped his face several times. Cleared his throat twice. "No, it's just, I never thought about it much."

"You didn't?" Joe sneered. "I've seen you kill some other things before. Kid's stuff. This is the real thing."

All of a sudden Sam smiled. An evil, hungry smile. Joe thought he looked like a monster. But the youth was putty in his hands now. The lure of excitement in raising the stakes was too much for Sam. He had nothing to lose. Didn't need much of a reason to act on his primal instincts. *Joe* would do the thinking for him. He would certainly take care of that problem. And if things ever did go bad, well, Sam was stupid enough to take the fall. His way out if it came to that.

"Okay. How are we gonna' do it?"

"We'll find some rope. Strangle her after we've had some fun."

Sam nodded like an obedient puppy. How pathetic, Joe thought.

"Then we'll burn the house to the ground. We'll be long gone, and everyone will think it was an accident."

"Yeah, burn it. Cool." Sam's nervousness had vanished completely. His look said everything—whatever Joe wanted, he was in. His slide into depravity had reached a new level. Everything was fair game. Anything and everything. Joe was absolutely right—Sam had nothing to lose anymore. It was all long gone.

"Wait here. I'm going out to the barn. She has to have gasoline somewhere, a container or something. I'll start pouring it inside so we don't have to worry about it later. She won't be back for a while. But keep your eyes open anyway until I get back."

"What if she *does* come back for some reason?"

Joe shook his head. "What do you think? Grab her and hold her down. Can you handle that?"

"Yeah."

Joe returned to the kitchen and tried the door, finding it locked. He soon had it open and he turned off his flashlight, not wanting to reveal himself to any chance cars passing by. So far, they'd yet to hear a single one since breaking in. The barn was a few dozen yards away and he hurried to reach it. The door was closed, but luckily unlocked. He entered, smelling chickens, and hearing them as well. The floor was covered with straw, a variety of tools neatly set on hooks against the wall. He jumped as one of them, a long shovel, gently swayed, as if pushed.

"Who's in here?" He tried to sound brave, but he was caught off guard. If someone was here, they would need to be dealt with...

He shined the light into every corner, but the place looked empty. There really wasn't any place to hide, except…Joe looked up.

The loft.

A ladder was set against a long, wooden post. He bit his lip, his own nervous habit. There was no choice—he had to check it out. His plans would be ruined if someone spotted them, although he had no idea who could be out here. Maybe an animal was loose, knocking the tool as it scurried around. He *hoped* that was the case.

Keeping his flashlight aimed high, he moved to the ladder, preparing for a confrontation. He brought out a long pocket knife and placed it between his teeth. Then he started working his way up, rung by careful rung, all the time his eyes darting around everywhere, searching for movement. The only noise was the occasional squawking of the birds, but nothing else materialized. He reached the top, cautiously poking his head over the rim. His light sliced across small bales of hay and wooden crates, but besides these, the loft was bare. There was nowhere someone could hide, and he breathed a bit easier. So he descended, convinced that the barn was empty, save for himself and the chickens. Maybe a cat was running around, spooked by his appearance. On his way down, he spotted a large plastic gasoline container. He walked over, still keeping his eyes open for anything unusual, and picked it up. The smell of gas was strong, and the container was nearly full. Exactly what he needed.

He carried it with him, the knife in the same hand. Joe wasn't taking any chances. Now back at the door, he set the gas down outside, and turned to shut the panel. His light flickered across the barn floor, and he snapped it back to the ladder in surprise. Were his eyes playing tricks on him? The ladder seemed to *ex-*

pand, as if it were being pulled slowly apart by powerful hands.

He gasped, clearly worried. Now it looked normal. What was going on? He swallowed heavily, keeping the flashlight's beam fixed on the ladder. Joe waited there, afraid to move, scarcely able to breathe. He refused to take his eyes off the ladder. Could it have been his imagination?

This place was weird. It gave him the creeps. He also felt an unpleasant sensation like he was being watched by someone. It wasn't something he could explain, and blame it on his nerves, maybe. But he couldn't shake the feeling. And he needed to get back to the house. Joe didn't trust Sam. He listened to orders, but beyond that…And this was no time for second-guessing or distraction. They couldn't afford mistakes tonight. Not if they wanted to get away with it.

With one last glance behind him, he shut the door, carrying the container. The night was quiet except for a stray cricket droning in the field to his right. Joe hustled across the lawn and was back inside in seconds. He made sure to lock the kitchen door, and then he called softly for Sam. "Hey, where you at?" The kitchen was empty, and Joe entered the dining room where he'd last seen him, but there was no sign of Sam anywhere.

"Idiot," Joe muttered. Now where *was* he? Probably upstairs. The bedroom, maybe. He scanned the floors and walls in every direction as he made his way through the house. There was nothing striking about the place, not a thing remarkable. To all intents, Pat lived a relatively simple life in her home. Joe still believed she kept secrets from the outside world though. Her family didn't just disappear one day, never to be found again, leaving no trace behind. The popular local opinion was that they had been abducted while the girl slept. No one really thought Pat had anything to do with it. A young teenage girl, with a happy home life, didn't go and kill her guardians for no reason, hide the evidence, and completely fool the authorities. In books and movies maybe, but not real life. And her other aunt had vanished as well, several years prior to the event. True, Pat was a small girl then, and it was a hard stretch to pin that one on her. But doubt nagged at Joe as he climbed the stairs, feeling the isolation of the house closing in on him. There was something very odd about everything. Pat might prove to be a greater challenge than he first thought. Not physically, of course. But he wouldn't be surprised to find, say, weapons of some type around. A gun or two. Something that would give her away. The proof was here, somewhere. In time, he might have discovered it.

Tonight though, he would have to hear the truth from the horse's mouth.

Joe splashed gasoline against the walls and poured some on the floor as well, making sure to hit as much as possible. He gained the stairs, cautiously making his way higher, still looking for his missing companion. He reached the top hallway, and looked down the corridor. His light passed over a small, square table holding a vase, and he saw several doors. The one at the end was open, most likely the bedroom. Good place to start. He approached, his boots clicking against the hardwood flooring. Halfway down the hall he stopped, hearing a louder noise, like floorboards creaking.

He spun around...

"Sam? That you?"

The hall was empty, the house lifeless. The creaking stopped, and he frowned, confused. He fingered his knife, and decided to keep it handy. Joe continued moving forward and reached the doorway, poking his head inside. There was the bed, but the place looked empty. He entered the room, probing his light into every corner. Nothing.

He checked the bathroom, finding only towels and neatly folded clothing.

Joe then went into each room, finally concluding that Sam was definitely not upstairs. And he wasn't on the first floor either...It would have been obvious. Where had he gone? He nodded to himself, already knowing the answer. The basement. Swearing under his breath, Joe hurried through the house, his anxiety reaching a new level. For the first time, he seriously considered calling the whole thing off, but just as quickly he shook the idea away, and descended into the basement, his beam cutting through the damp murkiness. Every sound now felt like an intrusion, his movements more uncertain with each passing step.

But the basement was empty too. Where the hell was he? He felt his heart pound in his chest. This was not as planned. When he caught up with his partner...

Joe turned around, ready to go back upstairs when he paused, remembered the cold cellar. A chill crept along his spine at the memory, and he waited for a moment. For some reason, the notion of entering that room bothered him. Maybe because Sam had claimed to see something strange in there. And Joe had seen—imagined—something weird in the barn. No way. The place was *definitely* getting to him. Nerves, man. He had to check everywhere for his friend. No time to waste.

Joe walked over to the door, calling. "Sam? Are you in there?" There was no reply, and with some reservation he turned the handle, shining his light inside, when he heard a loud noise from upstairs, freezing him instantly.

It was the strangest thing he ever heard...

Like something was ready to snap, bent to the breaking

point. It had to be Sam, but what could he possibly be doing up there? And where had he been? There were no answers for him down here, so Joe raced through the basement, bounding up the steps two at a time. Sam needed a good ass-kicking for sure. Joe stormed into the kitchen, but he stopped short, viewing a scene which terrified him to his very bones…

The house had changed.

The walls were shifted, molded in some impossible way, as if melted in an inferno. The paneling rippled and oozed like thick liquid.

And the table *moved*. The legs were animated, bending and thrashing in every direction.

Joe screamed at the top of his lungs and ran…

He burst into the dining room, his light held frantically before him. And to his growing horror, he saw movement in here as well. The floorboards at his feet whipped about, freed from their nails, and smacked against him, bruising his shins. Almost falling, he caught himself on the dining room table and something grabbed him back. He pulled away in revulsion, thinking only of escape. Crashing through the center, he tumbled headlong and fell hard on the floor, rolling until he regained his balance once more. The house was a living thing, full of creaks, scratching noises, and other sounds he dared not think about.

The living room appeared no different. Above the fireplace, the mantle writhed like a snake. In the far corner the rocking chair slammed repeatedly back and forth, back and forth, as if some invisible lunatic was trying to see how fast he could go. Joe reached for the door but withdrew in pain, watching in fascination as thin, crooked fingers emerged from the dull wood, flexing as if they were the stiff, arthritic joints of an old man. He heard a deep, booming sigh, which seemed to come from everywhere and nowhere.

It was nightmarish, terrifying beyond belief. All thoughts emptied from his mind except that he needed to get out of there *now*. In a desperate move, he braced himself, and leaped through the front window. He winced in pain as glass shredded his face and arms, but he made it, rolling sideways and landing against the railing. He raised himself on hands and knees, his vision blurred from terror-sweat and blood. Unable to catch his balance yet, he remained there for several seconds, then realized that the porch was trembling, preventing him from standing.

The floorboards opened up, closing about his legs in an unbreakable grip. He struggled, fighting with all his strength, but it was no use. By the second, he felt himself being impossibly drawn into the wood, absorbed, and his skin felt as if thousands of biting insects were crawling over his flesh. The house heaved and thrashed about him, like a great beast fighting the shackles which held it.

Joe's body was consumed, his head the only part left exposed. He blinked, trying to understand what was happening to him, his consciousness quickly fading.

And with his last flicker of breath, he finally knew where Pat's family had gone.

To anyone else it would have sounded cliché, but Pat was enjoying the time of her life.

Tim returned, carrying the drinks. The apple cider was warm and soothing, with just enough cinnamon to complete its perfection. She absolutely loved it. In a few minutes, their appetites led them to the main table, where they piled on servings of beef goulash, sloppy goblins, pumpkin soup, and a host of other side dishes. Pat thought it was a feast. To Tim's delight, the girl opened up remarkably, talking more, and returning polite greetings from a number of local folk who recognized her. They dug in, sharing a few bites, when Mayor Grimley approached, slapping Tim on the back and making him cough up a chunk of hamburger roll.

"Ah-ha, you made it here anyway. *And* with a date, I see. Well…Who might this adorable young girl be?"

"I'm Pat Kucher, we met a few years ago when I was in high school. I remember you came to an assembly on safety."

The mayor paused, several expressions clouding his face, finally stopping with a mixed look of surprise and sadness. "Why, so it is. Pat…Glad to see you. How are you, honey?"

She nodded, giving a slight smile. "It's a great dance. My only regret is that I've missed the last few."

"Well Tim better make sure it doesn't happen *again*. You've got a live one here, Patty. Half the farmer's daughters in the county are looking to sink their greedy little fingers into this boy. He's a heartbreaker." Mayor Grimley wagged a scornful finger at him, and Tim blushed in response, hoping the dim lighting concealed his embarrassment at the gross exaggeration. Pat was all smiles though.

"He was always nice to me in school. It's been, well…a bad spell for me the past few years. I hope it's over now."

"I understand. Really I do. If you ever need anything at all, just ask, girl. I'll take care of you. I *am* the mayor, you know. Well, I'll leave you two in peace for a bit. And get out there and dance. Don't be shy."

He gave a knowing wink at Tim and was off, doing a side-step shuffle which brought loud laughter from a group of people further down the table. The band was kicking in at high speed now, in the middle of a raucous crowd pleaser, a bellowing country piece which was all over the FM lately, although Pat didn't know the name of the song or the band. Something about farmers and whiskey…Nonsensical lyrics, but good fun. The melody was sprightly, the tune already a modern dance hall standard. Pat stared at the dancers, with a sidelong glance at Tim. Did he want to dance?

Pat reconsidered, staring at the dessert table, and decided she wasn't quite ready for the dance floor just yet. She stared at the chocolate cupcakes, which looked simply divine. "Tim, could you…"

She never finished her sentence. From the corner of her eye, she watched in horror as a slight bulge appeared along the wall near the back of the hall only a few yards away. Nobody else had noticed except Pat, but that was the purpose. It was meant for *her* eyes alone. Something she hoped never to see, her worst fears materialized. A sign of *activity*.

It was happening again.

Tim stared at her in confusion. "What is it? Are you all right?"

Pat closed her eyes, unwilling to look over at the corner. It was enough, she didn't need to see more.

Her keepers had awakened.

"I don't feel so good all of a sudden, I think it's something I ate. I need to get back home right away."

Tim looked devastated. "Did I say something wrong?" He shook his head, his face etched with concern. At that moment, he appeared incredibly vulnerable to Pat. Her heart ached as she watched him. So willing to listen and understand…No. She couldn't allow him to be hurt. He was already in danger, and knew nothing about it.

She stood. "It's not you, believe me. Let's go." She was already heading for the door. He quickly followed, and their hasty departure went unnoticed by the loud revelers as people were still coming in, others stepping outside to smoke. Pat hurried to the entrance, ignoring someone dressed as a toilet paper mummy who waved at her. Tim was on her heels, grabbing the door handle. They entered the night, behind them the band playing *Harvest Moon* by Neil Young. The women outside were still carrying on, and now were passing around their own spirits with a bottle of liquor.

"Good night," one of them called. "Beware the Headless Horseman."

Pat walked quickly with head bowed while Tim followed wordlessly. He didn't have time to open the door to his truck as she was already strapped in with her seat belt. He cranked the engine, backing carefully out of the parking lot, silent..

"It's not you, Tim. Please believe me."

It's closing in on me again.

"Hey, I just want to make sure you feel okay. It's all right, really."

No it's not.

The drive back to her place wasn't far, but time dragged. Pat looked out the window, her hands shaking.

Not again. I'm going to fight back this time. I won't let them destroy my life anymore.

When they finally arrived a few minutes later, there was little to say. Tim looked over at her, his eyes speaking for him. But she couldn't accept their quiet offer.

"Well, can I call you, to see how you're doing?"

She wanted that so badly, but shook her head. "No..." Her voice was husky with emotion. "Thank you, Tim. I had the best time in years. But I *have* to go. Now. Good-bye." Pat touched his hand, just for a moment, and then walked away. She felt his eyes following her, watching every step.

"Good-bye, Pat," Tim said, his voice barely registering over the engine's low hum.

And that was it.

The girl moved silently towards the house, a wraith that might never have existed. Pat reached the porch and unlocked the front door, entering quickly.

Everything appeared normal, but she was instantly assaulted by the acrid smell of gasoline, overwhelming her. The place stank of it. Gasoline? Where had that come from?

Something had happened here...There was no doubt. The activity at the dance wasn't brought on by her lashing out earlier then. And probably not by her leaving the house—she was only gone for an hour. But what was going on? The living room was as always, the cold stone of the fireplace the visual centerpiece in this part of the house, the rocking chair motionless in the corner. But the gasoline smell was powerful, as if someone had spilled a large amount. It didn't make any sense. She needed to understand what had taken place here, and figure out her next move. She was not going to be a helpless pawn any longer.

Unless it would keep Tim from harm...

Pat felt the walls closing in on her. Again. But she was above feeling the unrelenting fear as before. It certainly lingered, but failed to immobilize her. Tim, though, was another concern. He hovered on the edge of this nightmare—*her* nightmare. Her battle, to win or lose. Too many of her loved ones were dead, and somehow it was all because of her.

And although she didn't know how or why, Pat felt somehow that she was close to the truth. But she was missing something important here...

Pat didn't bother taking off her coat but she threw her purse onto the sofa, turning on a lamp and hurrying across the room. Then she saw it. On the floor, what looked to be a shard of glass. It was not there earlier, she was sure of it. And then she watched in disbelief as the fragment moved slowly across the flooring with a life of its own. Dread filled her as the impossible happened before her eyes. The glass slid up the sofa and molded itself into the front window into a small gap which she'd failed to notice.

The window was whole again.

The activity had returned in full force.

And something had occurred here while she was away...

Pat scrambled into the dining room now, and the smell was stronger yet. Turning on the overhead light, she spotted several things immediately out of place—the table was shifted, where it had been perfectly straight before. Two dinner plates were on the floor. She shook her head, bewildered.

Then it dawned on her. Someone had broken into her house!

That had to be it!

For whatever reason, burglary most likely, somebody entered after she was gone, and the house had awakened. And then what? Would they have been permitted to leave? With a sinking feeling, she already knew the answer—they were dead. They'd made a terrible mistake in choosing this house. *Her* house.

She slumped against a chair, trying to unravel the events. But what was she missing? The clue which would tie everything together? And what if, by chance, someone was still alive in the house? Was there more than one person involved?

Pat doubted it...Besides the piece of broken glass, everything else seemed normal once more. But she needed to be sure, so she headed upstairs, going from room to room, making certain that the place was empty. There were no signs of entry anywhere, however. Whether that meant the intruders had never gone upstairs, or left things untouched, she couldn't tell. Shortly, she made her way back down, deciding to check one last place—the basement. It had been a long time since she'd been down there, a few years. The basement still held terror for her, and she knew why, although the memories were always pushed aside when they surfaced.

Maybe it was time to face her past again. She *must* go down there. She felt strongly that it would reveal the answers she searched for, however terrible they might be.

And when she reached for the handle, she knew immediately the trespasser had entered that way. The lock was broken, and looked different in some way, the proportions all wrong. The lock had been *fixed* somehow, but…altered. And she didn't care to dwell on the matter. She turned the light switch on, and spotted several other things out of place. Boxes were scattered about, some of their contents sitting on the floor. Pictures.

She shuddered, remembering the weird anomalies which had shown up in the photographs. Visual signs that something extraordinary was happening around her, although her aunt and uncle had blamed it on their old camera.

Pat descended, ignoring the scattered pictures. She didn't need to see them again. The images were already graven forever into her memory. Instead, she walked straight to the back of the basement, stopping at the cold cellar, where her darkest memories waited patiently for her return.

Where it had all begun.

Tim waited until Pat entered the house, making sure she got in all right.

Her swing of moods was baffling. The night was going smoothly—he'd felt a real, honest connection with the girl. And her eyes…They didn't lie. Pat had been genuinely happy, telling him how wonderful it was to be out again. With *him*.

Could he have misjudged her that terribly?

No. He didn't believe it for a minute. Something had happened to Pat which changed her dramatically. But for the life of him, he had no idea what it was. His feelings were badly hurt, but the more he thought about it, the stranger everything appeared. It wasn't anything he'd done. Played the perfect date, been polite, hung on her every word, watched her reactions to the event. Gave her the music box, which she'd never even opened.

Then what was it?

Lost in thought, he sat in his truck, letting it idle in the street. He kept staring at the house, hoping that Pat would burst outside, run over to him, explain everything. But it seemed an empty wish. Maybe in romantic books and movies, his favorite comparison, but the real world? Yeah, to other people, not *him*. Self-pity washed over him now. He never had asked for much. Considering the tragedy of his parents, he'd still come out on top. His only real dream was to share his life with someone he cared deeply about.

Pat was the one for him.

He didn't care to look elsewhere. In subtle ways, maybe through their mutual losses, he felt bound to her. He pitied her terribly, and wanted to comfort the girl, who even admitted how lonely her own life was. So *what* exactly had happened? Tim placed his hands across his face, rubbed his eyes. Leaned his head back, and stared through the windshield.

Stars were out on this Halloween night.

He reached out with one hand, pretending to pluck one from the sky.

"This one's for you, Pat." His voice was a husky whisper. "I know I'm not the brightest guy around, or the richest, or best looking..."

He closed his fist tight around the imaginary gift. If this was what love felt like, he was better off being alone. He didn't want this kind of pain in his life.

"I could have loved you. Well, I think I already do." He paused. "Pat, I would give you my life, I think, just to make you happy. I really would. I hope you enjoy your present at least, and remember me. And don't ever stop dreaming..."

He sighed, feeling his eyes moisten.

"C'mon, you dumb farmer. Don't be getting sentimental now. Things don't always work out like you want. *You* of all people should know that by now. Mom and dad would tell you to pick yourself up and move ahead. That's what life's all about, anyway. But I guess I can still wish..."

He put the truck into gear, ready to finally call it a night, convinced Pat wouldn't be coming outside. The chapter was closed. Maybe another day would prove different, but he had a strong premonition that somehow the two of them were just not meant to be. Rubbing his eyes again, he spotted something crumpled up in the middle of the road. He put the vehicle in park, deciding to see if it had been dropped from a passing car. He also hoped that it *didn't* belong to Pat. He had no desire to see her right now. It was too much disappointment for one day already…Maybe one lifetime.

Tim walked over to the spot, and saw that it was a wallet. "Don't want to lose that." He patted his own pocket, although he knew it wasn't his. He opened it, feeling a bit uncomfortable searching a stranger's property, but how else would he identify the owner? There had to be a driver's license or something inside.

He found it immediately, but he felt chills run along his skin when he recognized the face and name on the picture.

Joe Harper…

Tim bit his lip and looked up. He'd seen Joe and Sam more than once parked close to Pat's house, wondering what mischief they were up to. Had seen the way Joe looked at Pat in school already. Tim was certain this was no coincidence, and he had a horrible feeling right now about Joe's intentions.

She was in danger…

Pat removed the rusted lock on the door. It seemed someone else had been here as well. But that couldn't be helped now. There was nothing she could do.

Pushing aside the dread which threatened to overwhelm her, she opened the panel, the hinges moaning in protest. The light from the basement spilled inside, seeping into cracks and corners, chasing the shadows. Her eyes went immediately to where the well sat, dark memories leaking upwards from its round black maw like the musty breath of the grave. *Here* waited the terrible truth. She knelt down on the cold, damp floor, just as she'd done years ago.

And Pat tried to take back the wish…

A little girl's fancy, playing make-believe in quick anger. How could she know the terrible form her request would take? How could anyone think such power would arise from a child's fears?

Aunt Trish. Pat had adored the woman, and she the same, fiercely loving her young niece, spoiling her rotten, looking out for her welfare. But like all close relationships, there were misunderstandings at times. Like when Trish had scared her with a ghost story, not realizing that Pat was terrible frightened, running into the basement and hiding from the monsters upstairs. Pat had hovered before the well, casting her wish.

Don't let anything ever get me.

And that was it.

A simple plea from the mouth of a child, against the most basic of fears. Then later on that same night, Pat had watched the impossible happen, as something terrible had taken her aunt from the back porch. She'd been stunned, too shocked to even move for hours, until she was found later by Margie.

The memories of that day had overwhelmed her, confused and frightened the little girl. And although too young to understand it, that had proved to be the beginning of a frightful sequence of events. The police said Trish vanished without a trace, either leaving for some unknown reason, or perhaps been abducted. But they didn't have any clues to track down the suspects. Things like this were rare, but they did happen.

But Pat knew otherwise—that something was in the house with her, watching. Tried to tell Uncle Ray and Aunt Margie, and like typical adults, they refused to listen. She was an impressionable young girl, who had lost her best friend. She would have problems dealing with the unfortunate tragedy. Eventually, time would heal the wound.

The wound became worse though.

Another incident had occurred years later, an argument, when Pat had grown angry about something in school, and she did the unthinkable—raised her voice, swearing at Ray. Pat had been more upset than she dreamed possible, and ran away in shame, fearing his wrath. But Ray, with a heart bigger than his head, came seconds later after her, yelling that it was all right. He knew she didn't mean it. Margie followed her husband, the two of them pounding on her door, wanting the girl to stop crying, come out and talk..

And when Pat heard the screams of terror, she *did* stop, waiting inside her room, immobilized by the fear of what lurked outside. She didn't even remember how long it was until she finally left her bedroom, but it was long finished. Her aunt and uncle were gone.

It was then she began to understand the terrible nature of what dwelt in the home, what she called her keepers, those that watched. *They* were part of the very structure of the place, materializing in small ways. And larger ways as well. She would come to recognize times of activity, and other periods of dormancy. But she'd never fully comprehended the truth of their purpose and origin…

Until now.

Pat had summoned them, and they came, but not to terrorize her. She had called them her keepers, imprisoning her, forbidding the girl to leave for very long, or go too far away. But they did indeed watch her.

As protectors.

If they perceived a threat against her, they reacted. No matter the actual intention. Or the person. They were judge.

Jury.

And executioners, grim and unforgiving...

She broke down now, realizing her worst fears. Their verdict was absolute, these terrible hidden things. No area of gray permitted. Aunt Trish had attracted their attention and had been considered a threat to Pat's safety.

And she'd been the first one taken.

Aunt Margie and Uncle Ray were next, years later. Peaceful, kind people. As Pat recalled, there had never been a real moment of argument between the three. Until the night they were taken...It all made sense now. It *was* Pat's fault, although how she could be blamed for summoning the monstrous entity was beyond comprehension. She had been a normal young child, full of love for her family and the world in general. Not overly imaginative...

That word struck a chord in her. Imagination. She used to picture her imagination as a friend, a tangible entity with a life and mind of its own.

What if...

Yes.

She'd brought it to life when casting that one, small wish. But with such powerful, catastrophic results. It was unexplainable as to how it happened. Or what the nature was of this *thing* which had been summoned. It simply existed. And that was enough. But could she undo it somehow?

She *had* to try.

Tim ran up to the porch, looking in the front window. The curtains were drawn, and it was impossible to see inside. He knocked on the door, and waited there. Several minutes had passed since Pat went in, and he had no idea where she might be. But Joe's wallet was in his hand—that much he *did* know, and this opened up a world of possibilities, all of them bad...Tim needed to find Pat and warn her. Or help her, if she was in danger. He continued banging on the door but the house remained silent. Leaping over the porch rail, he looked at the side windows, but everything was dark, curtains drawn all around. He tried the back door, and found this to be locked as well. He felt time was running out, and a terrible sense of urgency struck him to do something. Tim looked around, finding a loose brick on the back patio. He smashed it against the window, then stuck his hand in, opening the lock. Pushing the door open, he stood in the kitchen, but no one was there. He caught a whiff of gasoline though, which reinforced his belief that Joe Harper, and most likely Sam Wixel with him, had been snooping around while they were at the dance, the two trouble-makers certainly up to no good.

"Pat!" He yelled. "Where are you? It's Tim!"

His calls went unanswered, and he burst into the dining room, ready for a confrontation.

But what Tim saw was *not* what he expected to see.

Not at all...

12

Pat stiffened, hearing the shouts from upstairs.

Horror squeezed her chest when she recognized that it was Tim, yelling for her. He was in the house!

Oh no, Tim, you don't understand!

She lifted herself off the ground and scrambled out of the cold cellar. "Tim!" She screamed, over and over, at the same time hearing his faint cries. She hurled herself across the basement, but stumbled over one of the pictures which had been pulled from a carton. She collapsed in a heap, tumbling to the ground, blacking out for a moment, and when she opened her eyes again, a photograph lay against her face. It showed herself as a young child with her Uncle Ray at the local fair. A big smile covered his face, but Pat's stare looked empty and lost as she sat stroking the mane of a small pony. And it could have been a trick of the flash, or a glitch in the film, but there was a black knob in the wood of the background stable, jutting out several inches near the ground.

Tim…

She pushed herself up from the basement floor, wincing at

the pain in her elbows and knees. In seconds she was on the steps and racing upwards. To her immense relief she heard Tim calling her name, but with a sinking sense of dread she recognized the shrillness in his tone, the overwhelming fear as his screams grew louder.

"No, no, *no!*" She cried out, smacking the walls with her bare hands as she crashed through the entryway and into the kitchen. "Let him alone! He's trying to help me!"

Her own calls went unanswered, and she entered the dining room, hearing a loud, gurgling noise like water being sucked down a drain. Pat made it just in time to see the vague outline of someone—*Tim*—being absorbed into the wall, crooked, monstrous fingers pulling him inside. His hand breached the surface for one lingering moment, and Pat grabbed it, holding on with everything she could.

"Tim…" She sobbed. "No, he's trying to help."

They locked hands for one brief moment, and then he was gone, the wall sealed over, Pat's hand smacking against normal wood. There was no sign of him. It was as if he'd never even existed. Pat slumped to the floor, defeated. She banged the walls with her open palms, ignoring the pain, demanding for Tim to be returned.

"Damn you…let him go! Let him go, please…"

The walls were silent—the house was silent, as she raged on.

Pat kept hitting the walls, over and over.

And over…

…and over…

…and over…

"Is that all she does?"

"Yeah, just stands and stares. Once in a while, if you get lucky, you see her running her hands across the walls, like she's searching for something. Weird. But, that's what severe trauma can do to some people. They never figured out what really happened that night. She burned down her house, several people missing. Not a trace left behind, no bones, nothing..."

"Ten years ago, right?"

"Yeah. Of all nights, Halloween. Maybe there is something special about that day."

"Well, I wouldn't go *that* far. The mind is still the greatest mystery of all. If we could only look inside someone's head—see what they see, think what they think, know what they know— that would solve everything."

"You really think so? We may not like what we find. It's an easy transition from dream to nightmare."

A pause.

"Why the window? Most with her condition have isolated rooms."

"Well, when we first brought her in, she still talked. She begged us for a view of the evening sky until we finally gave in. She never misses a sunset, and always holds that music box against her heart. No harm done."

"Hmm...I wonder why she does that?"

"I don't know, maybe she still dreams. That was the last time she ever spoke."

They both stared at the woman as she ran fingers over the window, the sinking sun spilling its final orange rays between the black iron bars and into the somber room. She looked outside, watching.

Waiting.

Hoping.
Pale fingers lifted the lid from the music box...

When you wish upon a star,
Makes no difference who you are,
Anything your heart desires,
Will come to you.

If your heart is in a dream,
No request is too extreme,
When you wish upon a star,
As dreamers do.

Fate is kind,
She brings to those who love,
The sweet fulfillment of their secret longing.

Like a bolt out of the blue,
Fate steps in and sees you through,
When you wish upon a star,
Your dreams,
come,
true...

THE WATCHING